Praise for Amanda McCabe
and her Regency Romances

"Thoroughly enjoyable."   —*Rendezvous*

"An extremely talented new voice that should find
an enthusiastic welcome from readers."
                          —Romance Reviews Today

"A lively, delicious Regency." —Karen Harbaugh

"Playful and passionate, sparkling and suspenseful . . .
first-rate entertainment."   —Diane Farr

A Tangled Web

Amanda McCabe

A SIGNET BOOK

SIGNET
Published by New American Library, a division of
Penguin Group (USA) Inc., 375 Hudson Street,
New York, New York 10014, USA
Penguin Group (Canada), 90 Eglinton Avenue East, Suite 700, Toronto,
Ontario M4P 2Y3, Canada (a division of Pearson Penguin Canada Inc.)
Penguin Books Ltd., 80 Strand, London WC2R 0RL, England
Penguin Ireland, 25 St. Stephen's Green, Dublin 2,
Ireland (a division of Penguin Books Ltd.)
Penguin Group (Australia), 250 Camberwell Road, Camberwell, Victoria 3124,
Australia (a division of Pearson Australia Group Pty. Ltd.)
Penguin Books India Pvt. Ltd., 11 Community Centre, Panchsheel Park,
New Delhi - 110 017, India
Penguin Group (NZ), cnr Airborne and Rosedale Roads, Albany,
Auckland 1310, New Zealand (a division of Pearson New Zealand Ltd.)
Penguin Books (South Africa) (Pty.) Ltd., 24 Sturdee Avenue,
Rosebank, Johannesburg 2196, South Africa

Penguin Books Ltd., Registered Offices:
80 Strand, London WC2R 0RL, England

First published by Signet, an imprint of New American Library,
a division of Penguin Group (USA) Inc.

First Printing, February 2006
10 9 8 7 6 5 4 3 2 1

Copyright © Ammanda McCabe, 2006
All rights reserved

 REGISTERED TRADEMARK—MARCA REGISTRADA

Printed in the United States of America

PUBLISHER'S NOTE
This is a work of fiction. Names, characters, places, and incidents either are the
product of the author's imagination or are used fictitiously, and any resemblance
to actual persons, living or dead, business establishments, events, or locales is
entirely coincidental.

The publisher does not have any control over and does not assume any
responsibility for author or third-party Web sites or their content.

Prologue

*D*iana Hillard had never been so excited in her life!

Her first masquerade ball. Well, first any sort of ball really. It was so unfair! Here she was, sixteen years old, and if her parents had their way she would be locked up in the nursery with her little sister Charlotte *forever*. Or until she made her bow in Town next year, which really amounted to the same thing. Two years was an eternity to be trapped in the country. She was wasting her youth here, when she longed to be dancing, going to the opera and the theater, flirting with handsome admirers.

Well—one admirer in particular. And the lovely thing was, she did not even have to travel to London to see *him*. He was right here. Waiting for her.

1

"Have a care, miss!" the mantua-maker's assistant said, her tone distinctly exasperated around the mouthful of pins. "If you keep moving about so the hem won't be straight."

"I'm sorry," Diana answered. She faced forward and resolved to stand statue-still, even as her feet longed to leap about. To dance! She could even now hear the musicians tuning up in the ballroom below her chamber, could hear carriages rolling their way down the drive. The ball was about to begin! And here she stood like a helpless porcelain doll, waiting for them to finish the last touches on her costume. Yet the woman *did* have a point. It would never do to appear with a crooked hem.

She gazed at her reflection in the full-length mirror that had been set up in her chamber for the fitting. The gown was lovely, quite the prettiest one she had ever possessed. It was just such a shame she could not dress as a shepherdess every day, for the tight bodice and full skirts suited her shorter, thin figure and made her look less girlish. The lace petticoats, glimpsed beneath the cutaway pink silk overskirt, rustled enticingly, and the ribbons trimming the square-necked blue bodice were very a la mode.

And to think, her parents had not wanted her to attend their masquerade ball! They had insisted she was far too young for such things, that they themselves were only giving the ball because their distant cousin, the Duke of Aston, and his son the Earl of Gilbert would be visiting and had to be amused properly. Diana had always secretly thought His Grace to be a great bore whose breath always smelled faintly of onions, but she blessed him now for causing this great event to occur. She also blessed the fact that her parents, though rather unreasonable about so many things, were susceptible to pleas and tears from their daughters. A few pitiful mews, some sobs, and *voila*! She was allowed to come to the ball.

But not the midnight supper. She was meant to retire before then, like a mere child. No matter. She had her *own* plans for later.

"There you are, miss! All finished." The assistant, her pins safely deposited in a dish, sat back on her heels with a satisfied smile. "And very pretty, too, if I may be so bold."

Diana gave her own smile at the girl in the mirror. She would have to agree. Maybe not *very* pretty, but definitely prettier than usual. She was under no illusions about her own charms. Her nose was upturned rather than Grecian, her cheeks plump and pink rather than poetically pale. And her hair—zounds! Her hair was the bane of her life, reddish-brown and wildly curling, not golden and shimmering like her sister's.

3

But on this night, in this gown, she looked—pretty.

If only *he* would agree.

There was no time to fret about that now, though. The ball was about to begin.

"Thank you all so much!" she cried, leaping down off the stool. She snatched up her hat, a fetching low-crowned, wide-brimmed creation of chip straw trimmed with blue and pink streamers, and tied it atop her upswept hair. Her maid waited at the door with her ribbon-bedecked shepherd's crook, and Diana caught it as she hurried out the door.

The curved heels of her shoes clicked and clattered as she dashed down the corridor toward the grand staircase, echoing the thrum of her heart. "First ball, first ball," it seemed to say. First ball—and he would be there! If he kept his promise. He *always* kept his promises.

Her parents waited to greet their guests at the foot of the stairs, her mother regal in black velvet and gold lace as Queen Elizabeth, her father rather incongruous as a Roman centurion. His bronze armor glinted in the glow of hundreds of candles, but could not quite disguise his portliness.

Diana took in a deep breath, clutching tightly to her crook. This was it—the beginning of her magical night.

Her mother glanced up and saw her hovering in the shadows at the top of the stairs. "There you are, my dear," she called. "Come down here at once, the guests are arriving."

"But don't run so, Diana," her father added sternly. "It is quite undignified for a young lady to run."

Diana walked in a very ladylike manner down the stairs to her mother's side. Lady Hillard gave her a quick glance, reaching out to adjust a bow there and frill here. Everything always had to be exactly perfect for Diana's mother, and Di found she so often fell short. She would usually prefer to be writing poetry in her own room, or telling Charlotte tales of the fairy folk, rather than pouring tea for the local gentry or perfecting an air on the pianoforte. Very often her mother would get this long-suffering frown on her lips when she looked at her eldest daughter. Yet Diana could hardly blame her. Lady Hillard took great pride in her family connections, in being a baronet's wife and a leader of the neighborhood. Rackety, bluestocking daughters had no place in such a scheme.

"You look very nice this evening, Diana," her mother said. "Does she not, Herbert?"

"Hm?" Sir Herbert Hillard glanced distractedly from the front door to his wife. *He* never noticed his daughters at all, except when they were doing something to embarrass him. Which was quite often. "Oh, yes, very nice. Now, Diana, only dance with the gentlemen on the approved list we gave you. Our cousin the duke; his son; the vicar . . ."

And on it went. Diana almost rolled her eyes at the hundredth mention of the "approved list." The onion-breath duke, his spotty son the earl, the ancient vicar. What a dreary evening *that* would be. If, that is, she had any intention at all of following The List.

She just gave her father a sweet smile, though, and said, "Of course, Papa."

"And it's up to your room you go before supper," he finished. The butler opened the door to admit the first group of guests, and there was no time for further lecturing.

It seemed hours before Diana could leave the reception line and actually enter the ballroom. She was escorted by her cousin, the spotty earl, who was prattling on about cricket or some such, as he always was. He was mad for sport. Even that could not dim her great pleasure at seeing the party laid out before her in all its splendor. The ballroom was usually kept shuttered and closed up; there had not actually been a ball there since Diana was a little child. But now the dim, dusty space was transformed.

Banks of emerald green potted plants had been

brought in and grouped along the yellow silk-papered walls. Flowers twined through the foliage, pink and white, their sweet scent heavy, mingling with the smoke of thousands of candles and the perfumes of the guests. A small orchestra played, hidden behind tall palms. Their tune was soft now, a slow, romantic ballad, but very soon they would strike up the opening minuet, and her parents would come to lead the dancing.

And the guests! Diana stared at them in wonder, her gaze darting from one to the other. They were quite transformed from familiar neighbors and visiting Town friends. She spied medieval knights, Eleanor of Aquitaine, Greek gods and goddesses, an angel, a devil, Harlequin and Columbine, even a bear in a shabby fur suit. They were a merry whirl of color and sparkle. Yet she did not see the one person she sought above all others.

A pang of disappointment pierced her transcendent joy. Next to her, Lord Gilbert tugged at her arm.

"Oh, I say, this *is* jolly," he said, his enthusiastic tone giving every indication that he was enjoying himself.

Diana glanced up at him. He was really not such a bad sort, despite being all sport-mad. He had nice brown eyes, and he did try to talk to her at breakfast and on walks. He was just not the one she looked for now. Longed for.

"Yes," she answered. "Very jolly."

"Would you dance the first set with me, Miss Hillard?" he asked, and she actually thought she could detect a blush spreading across his plump, sunburned cheeks. How very odd.

"Thank you, Lord Gilbert. That would be nice," she said. After all, he was on The List, and she *did* want to dance. While she waited for *his* arrival.

The dance proved to be "nice," indeed. Lord Gilbert was not a terrible dancer, and Diana did enjoy performing the steps she had practiced so carefully with the dancing master, with her sister Charlotte as partner. Lord Gilbert, at least, was taller than Charlotte, and the music was very fine. They moved without incident through the smooth patterns of the old-fashioned minuet and the lively reel that followed. At its conclusion, he escorted her properly to one of the gilt chairs set about the room and gave her a bow.

"Shall I fetch you a glass of punch, Miss Hillard?" he asked, tugging at his too-tight cravat.

"Yes, thank you, Lord Gilbert," Diana answered. She did not stay in her seat long after he dashed off on his errand, though. The music made her feet tap impatiently, and she had no good view of the crowd. She soon collected her crook and departed on an amble about the periphery of the room.

The crowds were not so dense closer to the walls, and Diana found a fairly clear pathway for searching the costumes and faces, the varied masks. He had promised he would be here!

As she passed a curtained alcove off one of the window seats, a hand suddenly shot out from behind the yellow satin drapery and clutched at her arm. She nearly screamed from the surprise, until a low, urgent voice whispered, "Don't shout out, Di! It's only me."

He was *here*! Just as he promised. She had been silly to think otherwise, even for a moment. Casting a quick glance about to be sure no one was watching, she ducked between the curtains and into his arms.

"Oh, Tom!" she whispered happily. Her crook fell to the floor as her arms twined about his neck. He smelled wonderful, of clean air and fresh soap and himself. She closed her eyes and inhaled deeply, as if to draw that perfect scent deep into her soul so she could never forget it. "You took an age."

His own arms came around her waist, holding her close. He was quite tall, and only the tips of her shoes touched the floor as she strained to be even closer. "I had to climb inside one of the li-

9

brary windows," he said. "Your butler won't let anyone by without an invitation written by your mother."

"Well, you're here now, that's all that matters, Tom. Oh, I have missed you so much!"

"You've been too involved with your grand guests, the duke and his son," he said. She could hear the mischievous grin in his dear, deep voice.

She pulled a face. "They *have* been demanding, always wanting to go for rides and play cards and such. They talk of nothing but hunting and shooting. It has been terrible, Tom. All the time I wanted only to be with you, in our hidden little spot. Where we could read poetry all day long and just be together." She could see it now, their sheltered grove in the woods, where they met to talk of the books they read, the dreams they had. To share a kiss or two. Or three. It was a perfect place, a heaven on earth.

"I've thought of nothing but you, Di," he said. "I wonder every moment what you're doing, what you're thinking about. I picture you reading in your library, or playing at your pianoforte, and I want only to see you for real. Every hour I will read a new poem or hear a funny jest, and I think, 'Di would enjoy this so much.' "

Her heart thrilled at his words. A warm glow spread through her veins to her very toes. He *did* care about her. Their times together were so short, so preciously fleeting, that she sometimes feared he forgot about her when she was not near. Now she knew he thought of her just as she did him.

"Oh, Di," he said, burying his face against her hair, knocking her hat askew. "This can't go on."

No, it couldn't. Not like this. She and Tom Cole were meant to be together. She had known that since the day they first met, when she lost her way on a long ride and stopped at a farmhouse for directions. It happened to be the house where Tom lived with his mother. His father had been a tenant of her father's, and Tom took over the farm when his father died, becoming the sole provider for his mother, even though he was just seventeen. That day, his mother gave her tea in their cozy sitting room, and then Tom himself led her home. She was immediately struck by how handsome he was, tall and strong, with waving, glossy black hair and bright sky-blue eyes. On their slow ride home, they talked of poetry. They had both read *Lyrical Ballads*, and they spoke of books and dreams, and the journey was all too short.

Since that day, they met as often as they could in their secret nook. Not nearly as often as Diana would like, of course. Tom did have to work, and she could not afford to arouse her parents' suspicions. They were determined she would make a grand splash in Town next year, and marry a marquess at the least. Diana did not want that, and never had. She wanted only a cozy, book-filled cottage with her Tom.

She stared up at him now in the shadows. The dim light fell over the sharp angles and planes of his face, the tumbled waves of his black hair, mussed by the half-mask he had shoved carelessly atop his head. He was so lovely, as if he could be a poet himself, racketing romantically across the Continent rather than being a sensible farmer in the Midlands. But all his good looks, his sense of family and responsibility, all would carry no weight with her parents if their meetings were discovered.

She shivered despite her joy, as if a black cloud passed over her glowing sun. Her hands clung tighter to Tom. Perhaps it had been a mistake to ask him here tonight, though she wasn't able to imagine her first real ball without him to share it.

"I have something for you, Di," he whispered.

"Something for me?" she answered, a spark of curiosity catching amid her trepidation. "A new volume of poetry?"

He grinned at her, his teeth white in the shadows. "You'll just have to wait and see."

"Wait?"

Tom glanced past her shoulder, and she suddenly became aware that the hum of conversation and laughter was growing louder, closer to their hidey-hole.

Her breath caught in her throat. They could not be discovered!

"Here, come with me," Tom said quickly. He pushed open the window in their nook, and swiftly climbed out onto the terrace. Diana couldn't help but giggle. She had never exited her own home through a window before! It seemed so illicit and romantic. Tom reached back to catch her around the waist and lifted her down in a flurry of skirts.

The terrace was lit by strings of festive Chinese lanterns, but no one was yet walking out there, luckily for Diana. No one saw their undignified appearance, or their mad dash down the steps into the dark garden. Hand in hand, they ran down the pathways until they came to a small clearing surrounded by tall hedges. A small summerhouse stood in the center, the moonlight shimmering on its copper roof, adding a touch of magic to the night.

As if any extra magic was needed, when she was with Tom! He twirled her around and around in a mad, improvised dance, making her laugh until she gasped helplessly, tears running from her eyes. He lifted her off her feet, spinning in a circle.

"Oh, Tom!" she cried, balancing her hands on his shoulders. "I wish tonight would never end. That we would always be together like this."

"I wish that, too," Tom said, slowly lowering her to the ground. Even though her feet touched earth, she still felt she twirled in the heavens.

"One day soon we will find a way," she said, as she had so many times before. One day, surely her schemes would find fruition and she and Tom would marry, with the full approval of her family. Surely if she just thought hard enough . . .

All thought was impossible, though, when Tom embraced her. His arms around her were so delightful she could contemplate nothing else. His lips found hers in the darkness, soft, insistent, and that kiss was her whole world. Just like in a poem.

"Oh, Tom," she whispered, as his lips slid away from hers.

"This is for you, Di," he said roughly. He took one of her hands, and she felt the cool press of metal against her palm. She glanced down and saw the moonlight gleam on a small, gold, heart-shaped locket suspended on a thin chain.

"Oh, Tom," she said again, breathless. "It's so beautiful."

"It belonged to my grandmother," he answered.

He took it from her hand and clasped it about her neck. The cool weight of it lay against her breastbone, solid and perfect—just like Tom's love.

Diana covered it with her hand. "If it was your grandmother's, it is too precious to give away," she protested, even though she knew she could never relinquish it.

Tom shook his head. "She would want you to have it—just as I do. When she gave it to me, she told me to gift it only to my true love."

She stared up at him in wonder, the locket warming under her hand. "Am I your true love, Tom?"

"You know you are, Di."

With a cry of utter joy, Diana launched herself back into his arms, pressing her lips to his in a kiss that contained all her wild love, her youthful ardor.

"What is the meaning of this!"

A stentorian voice, full of outrage and fury, rang across the clearing, destroying in the lash of six words the magic, iridescent bubble of Di's moment. She jerked away from Tom, spinning around to see her father standing at the edge of the summerhouse.

Earlier, she had thought his Roman centurion garb faintly comical. It was not comical in the least now. He looked like an avenging Caesar, as if he would draw his pasteboard sword and run Tom through. Indeed, his fist closed convulsively over the gilded hilt, a vein pulsing dangerously in his forehead. He was utterly furious, and all her vague hopes of finding a way to reconcile her family to her hoped-for marriage to Tom vanished.

She trembled again, but not with joy or passion. She felt a quaking fear unlike any she had ever imagined before. She reached out blindly for Tom's hand, which clasped hers in a warm, steady grip, giving her a measure of courage.

"P-Papa," she managed to stammer out. "I did not see you there. . . ."

"That much is obvious, Diana," her father boomed. "You were too busy disgracing yourself with this farmer! I told your mother you could not be trusted at a ball, that you were too headstrong, too lacking in any good sense."

"Papa!" Diana protested, stung. "That is not true."

"Of course it is true! I have just been proved right, in a most shocking fashion. What if someone had seen you? You almost disgraced us all with your reckless and wanton behavior."

He strode forward to grab Diana's arm, tearing her away from Tom and marching her so smartly away from him that her feet barely touched the ground. She gave a strangled, inarticulate cry of protest, struggling to twist around so she could see Tom.

"Diana, no!" Tom shouted. She heard the swish of his cloak, the click of his boots on the gravel. "Sir Herbert, it is not what . . ."

"Silence!" her father yelled, whipping around to face Tom. Diana was dragged along with him, and she caught a glimpse of Tom's strained, desperate face, his clenched fists. "You have abused my generosity to your family, assaulted my daughter, you ungrateful whelp! I will deal with you later. And if you follow us now and cause a scene, it will go all the worse for you—and especially for *her.*"

He pulled Diana along behind him as he hurried back through the garden and up the servants' staircase. Diana scarcely registered the shocked glances of the servants, the speculative murmurs. Her head was spinning with the swiftness of discovery, the threats against her love—the fear of what would happen next.

She tried to extricate herself from her father's grasp, to protest, but he cut her off at every turn, shaking her arm to silence her. When they reached her chamber, he pushed her inside, his face set in irreversible lines of doom.

"You stay here," he hissed. "You will mend

your wanton ways now, Diana. We will not let you ruin this family with your headstrong behavior."

Then he slammed the door in her face, and she heard the grate of a key turning in the lock. She was trapped!

Diana fell against the stout, unyielding wood, pounding at it with her fists, sobbing. No one came, of course, and she eventually collapsed to the floor in an exhausted heap, the skirts of the gown she had taken such pride in only hours before crumpled around her.

"Oh, Tom," she murmured tearfully, clutching at her locket. "What have I done?"

It was four days before Diana could escape from the house, and the watchful eyes of her parents, to make her way to the house Tom shared with his mother. She ran as quickly as she could over the lanes and fields, breathless, desperate, only to find the cozy farmhouse shuttered and empty. She dashed from window to window, going up on tiptoe to peer through the wavy glass. The furniture was shrouded in holland covers, all the pictures and figurines gone.

A passing farmworker strolling down the lane told her what had happened.

"The Coles immigrated," he said, watching her

curiously. She didn't even care what gossip her distraught state might give rise to. "Or so I heard. The squire visited them, and they packed up and left the very next day."

"Immigrated?" Diana said, aghast.

"To British North America, I think. They sold all their livestock and such."

The man went on his whistling way, and Diana took off for the forest glade where she used to meet Tom. Surely he left something for her there, a note or token, saying where he had gone and when he would come back for her. But there was nothing. Only heavy, green silence where there had once been so much laughter.

He had left. He had not even cared enough to fight for her, or tell her to wait for him.

She cried that day, falling down on the soft grass to sob out all the heartache of first love, first loss. Finally, when the light turned pale and rosy at the edges of the sky, she drew herself wearily to her feet and walked home. A week later she went to stay with her aunt, Lady Ransome, until she could have her Season, which ended in her wedding to the Earl of Gilbert and a honeymoon to Scotland where he could fish and shoot. She never cried over Tom Cole again.

But she never lost her locket, either.

Chapter One

Twelve Years Later

"*I* am bored."

Miss Bourne, companion to Mary, Lady Ransome, barely glanced up from her embroidery. She had been with her ladyship for several years now, and she was accustomed to such outbursts. "Oh, yes, my lady?"

"Yes," Lady Ransome answered firmly.

Miss Bourne sighed. These flights usually meant more work for her, in one way or another. They had enjoyed a peaceful few months. It was time for some upheaval. She was resigned to it. "And what do you propose to alleviate this boredom?"

"I am glad you asked," Lady Ransome said happily. She sat back in her tapestry armchair, set conveniently beside the fire laid after their supper. A blanket covered her legs, drawn up over her purple silk skirts so the myriad of cavorting lap dogs would not stain them. A lace cap perched on her soft white curls, and a book lay open on the arm of her chair. She looked the very picture of a genteel lady of advanced years, having a bit of a read before she retired. Miss Bourne, though, knew that was not true. The faded blue eyes, the silk-covered plumpness, the doting on her small dogs concealed a spirit of irrepressible restlessness.

The rest of them could only trail along in her wake.

"I propose to have a party," Lady Ransome answered.

"A party?" Miss Bourne said, bewildered. Whatever she had been expecting—and she thought herself prepared for anything—it was not that. Ransome Park had not seen a party since Lord Ransome died fifteen years ago. They were too isolated. "You mean a ball or something? Who would we invite, beyond the neighbors?"

"Not a ball." Lady Ransome shook her walking stick in the air, sending her dogs into paroxysms of barking. "My dancing days are far behind me. I thought a house party. Some people in for a few days."

"A house party, my lady?" Miss Bourne asked. That did sound like a great deal of work.

"You needn't look as if I propose inviting in the Mongol hordes! Just a few friends, to liven things up a bit. It was such a dreary winter. We deserve some fun, don't you think?"

Fun? That wasn't what Miss Bourne would call it. But she knew her duty. She reached for the portable writing desk that was never far away. "Whom do you propose to invite, my lady?" she said, taking out paper and a pencil.

"Hm, now, let me see." Lady Ransome began ticking off names on her beringed fingers, while Miss Bourne lagged behind, writing it all down. "My dear niece Diana, of course, Lady Gilbert. She has launched her sister Charlotte into Society this last Season, and I have not seen either of them in an age. Not since Diana's husband's funeral. Invite them. And some young people for Charlotte, so she doesn't expire of boredom amongst us old folks. Now, who could . . ."

"Is not Miss Hillard friends with Lady Caroline Reid, my lady?" Miss Bourne suggested.

"Excellent memory, Miss Bourne! Yes, Lady Caroline, daughter of the Earl of Burton. Put her on the list. And a couple of young gentlemen. It could never hurt to try a spot of matchmaking while they're here, since both ladies ended their

Season unbetrothed." Lady Ransome closed her eyes, trying to recall young sons and grandsons of her acquaintances who were not of too rakish a reputation. "Did I not read that Lady Caroline was seen about in the company of Roland Kirk-Bedwin during the Season?"

"Yes, indeed. A betrothal was expected, according to the *Morning Post*, but was never forthcoming."

"Now, *that* sounds interesting. Put Mr. Kirk-Bedwin down, and his friend, Lord Edward Sutton. He is the youngest son of a duke, you know, and has at least ten thousand a year. He might do very well for Charlotte."

Miss Bourne did like the way Lady Ransome's mind worked. "Excellent idea. Who else?"

"I suppose we must have that new widow who is lodging at Everly Abbey. She had me to dinner and cards last week, and I must reciprocate, though a house party seems a bit much."

"Mrs. Elizabeth Damer?"

"Yes. Mrs. Damer. A rather charming lady, though perhaps a bit—hard. Oh, well, she might be company for Diana, they are almost of an age. And Mr. Frederick Parcival from the Grange. A first-rate card player, which is always helpful after dinner and on rainy afternoons."

"That makes seven, my lady."

"Almost full. I can't abide crowded house parties. One can't talk with everyone. We must ask my new friend Mrs. Rachel Cole. She and I have such interesting conversations, and she will keep me company while the young people go off on their own activities. And I hear that her son Thomas is visiting her. We must ask them. That will do it, I think."

Miss Bourne studied her list. Two nieces, a social butterfly, two noblemen, a widow who was perhaps a bit of an adventuress, a card player, an elderly widow with a son who had lately grown very wealthy in the North American fur trade. A most interesting party indeed. Perhaps her task would not be so onerous after all.

Elizabeth Damer sat at her dressing table, studying the invitation from Lady Ransome. A house party at Ransome Park. *How very—singular*, she thought, turning the heavy parchment over in her hand. She had invited Lady Ransome to her first dinner party here at the crumbling, drafty old Abbey, of course. The old lady was the greatest social personage in the neighborhood. They had gotten along well enough, certainly. But she had considered that the difference in their stations and ages would prevent them from becoming friends. Not to mention the difference in their *incomes*.

25

Elizabeth dropped the invitation atop the vast mound of bills that had come in the morning post. Dressmakers, milliners, furriers, jewelers, carriage makers, grocers—they had pursued her from Town even to this secluded corner of countryside where she tried to take refuge. Their letters were rude in the extreme, threatening such indignities as debtors' prison. As if they had not received more than a return on their investment by having their pitiful wares seen being worn and driven by a lady of her beauty and stature!

With a low cry, Elizabeth swept the bills off the table. They fluttered down like snow, landing on her new pink carpet. She cursed Andrew roundly, and not for the first time. When they wed, he promised her wealth, a life of ease and fashion where she would never have to work or worry again. She would just have to be his wife. She had not really liked Andrew—he was too short, too bald, too unexciting a lover. But his promises won her over, and she married him—only to find he hadn't a bean to his name. Everything had to be purchased on credit to maintain their lifestyle.

Then he dared to die! Killed in a duel by a jealous husband, the stupid sot. And the creditors closed in on her, forcing her to flee the joys of London for this pitiful backwater where no one appreciated how very au courant her clothes were, how beautifully she styled her carefully golden hair, how she condescended to talk to them.

She glanced in the mirror to admire that hair, but was suddenly caught by a much more mundane sight. A *line* marring her alabaster skin near one green eye.

"No!" she shrieked, covering that offending flaw with her hand. It could not be!

Time was running out. She had to do something drastic, and soon. Her gaze fell on Lady Ransome's invitation. It was her only hope now. There had to be at least one rich bachelor at this party who was in search of a pretty wife. A wife he longed to keep in luxury.

There just had to be.

Frederick Parcival stared down at the invitation he had laid next to his breakfast plate, chewing his eggs thoughtfully as he contemplated the fact that he was being summoned to Ransome Park.

This was a surprise. He knew Lady Ransome a bit, of course. In such a small neighborhood, everyone was acquainted with everyone else. He had last seen her when they were both dining at the Abbey with the beauteous Mrs. Damer. But he would not have thought he would be asked to a house party at Ransome Park. *She* was Countess of Ransome; he was the younger son of a baronet, run out of Town by gaming debts and his own exhaustion.

Ah, well. Perhaps she needed an extra man to make up the numbers. He was always useful for that. And it might be worth his while. There was bound to be a card game or two, and he had heard that Lady Ransome had a niece, a rich young widow. She could quite possibly make an appearance there.

Yes—worth his while indeed. Frederick laid the invitation aside and cut into his sausages with great gusto. A rich widow could set him to rights in no time.

"So, are you going to this do at Ransome Park, Edward?" Roland Kirk-Bedwin asked, reaching for the bottle of wine. He and his friend Lord Edward Sutton were dining at the club before deciding what to do for the rest of the evening. It was quiet in Town now that the Season had officially ended. Even the club was only half full, bored young men eating their suppers or perusing the papers by the fire, a few desultory games in the billiards room.

Roland was bored. Restless. As if he longed for something, something he could not quite define or name. But he was filled to the brim with it.

Edward watched him from behind the oval

lenses of his spectacles, calm as always. He was a good friend to Roland, one of the few who did not seek to lead him back into the sinkholes of the brothels and gaming hells—sinkholes Roland was hard-pressed not to happily fall into. But he had to think of his ill mother, of how he was her only support now. She worried about him so much. Every time he visited her in her country cottage, she told him tearfully of another newspaper story she had read of his wild exploits in Town. She begged him to go to his uncle, who would make him his heir and set him up in a parish if he would only take orders—him, a churchman! Or she urged him to find "a nice young lady" and settle down with her. A nice, *rich* young lady, of course.

He had thought he found one, during the Season. Thought he found a young lady of not only respectable fortune but great beauty and bright spirit. He and Lady Caroline Reid would dance together at balls, race their horses through the park (much to the chagrin of more sedate equestrians!), and laugh over teas and suppers and cards. She was such a mischievous spirit, so merry and glorious, with her bright red hair and gleaming blue eyes. She was all he could have hoped for in a lady. And if there was some undefinable something missing in his feelings for her, well, surely that would grow in time. It was either her or the church.

He was prepared to make his declaration when she suddenly dropped him. No explanation, no warning. Just a cool snub at a ball, then silence. Until she left Town at the end of the Season, and the papers came out with a gleeful flurry of articles detailing his downfall with "the glorious Lady Caro."

Roland was still reeling. Reeling and—angry.

Edward blinked at him. "The Ransome house party?" he said. "Oh, yes, very possibly. The house is a fascinating case of remade medieval architecture I would love to study. And Lady Ransome is a friend of my mother, she would ring a peal over my head if I didn't go. Also, there's not much going on here for a few more months, is there? No lectures at the Medieval Society, and as for the pitiful new exhibit at the British Museum . . ."

Roland laughed, and tossed back the last of the wine. He gestured to the footman for a fresh bottle. "Oh, Edward! Is that all London means to you? Lectures and museums?"

"Of course not. There is Almack's and things of that ilk."

"I see we have our work cut out for next Season." Roland grinned at Edward. Yes, Edward

Sutton was a bit of a stick in the mud, but he was really a good chap. He had rescued Roland from numerous scrapes over the years. Edward was just very smart, far more intellectual than Roland could be or wanted to be, and he needed Roland's help to find the lighter side of life.

Edward ignored his admonitions to forget museums and Almack's, as he always did. He just cut another bite of his chop and said, "So, you are also invited to Ransome Park?"

"I certainly am."

"Are you going? We could drive down together, if you like."

"That would be excellent, Edward. Your carriage is far better sprung than mine, y'know."

Edward slowly chewed and swallowed, watching Roland thoughtfully. He took a careful sip of wine before saying, "Charlotte Hillard is Lady Ransome's niece."

"Is she?" Roland said, wondering what possible interest this information could have for him. He could hardly recall what Miss Hillard looked like, a thin blonde who had a fine dowry, perhaps, but was very quiet.

"Yes. And, as you remember, Miss Hillard is very good friends with Lady Caroline Reid. They go everywhere together now, so I hear."

Roland paused in lifting a forkful of greens to

his mouth, staring at Edward. Shocking, what an affect even hearing her name still had for him. "Indeed?"

"So I hear," Edward said again. He took another sip of wine. "Still want to go to Ransome Park?"

Chapter Two

"*W*ill there be very many people there, do you think?" Charlotte Hillard asked quietly, her large green eyes peering worriedly out the carriage window at the hedgerows that flew past.

Diana glanced up from her book, her mouth open to answer her sister, but Lady Caroline Reid spoke first. "Oh, pooh, Charlotte, of course there won't be very many people there! It's a country house party, not Vauxhall. You needn't be frightened."

"I'm not *frightened*," Charlotte protested. "I just—wondered."

Diana gave Charlotte a gentle smile. Her sister had a sweet, shy nature, quite in contrast to her outgoing bosom bow Lady Caroline, who chat-

33

tered and laughed like a flamboyant redbird. Charlotte preferred to stay at home with Diana in their Portman Square townhouse, which had been their residence since the deaths, in shockingly quick succession, of their parents and Diana's husband. Even though their house was in the midst of Society, and Diana herself enjoyed company on occasion, Charlotte liked to be quiet, spending her evenings with a book or a few close friends. It made her close friendship with Lady Caroline a bit mystifying, but Diana did not mind it. She had hopes that Lady Caroline would help Charlotte emerge from her shell.

A country house party, with mostly family and people Charlotte knew, seemed a good place to begin. She seemed nervous about even that. At least she *looked* lovely, with her smooth, silvery blond hair coiled beneath a stylish straw and pale green silk bonnet. Her sea-green eyes were set off by a darker green pelisse. She was so fortunate to have inherited their mother's blond beauty, rather than their father's brown hair and eyes, as Diana herself had. As a girl, Diana had despaired of her unfashionable looks. Now, they hardly mattered. She was a respectable widow who need no longer concern herself with such frivolities.

If someone would just tell her vain heart that!

"It will be nice to see Aunt Mary again," Diana

said. "And I'm sure she will not have invited anyone who could make you in the least bit uncom-
fortable, Charlotte."

"Yes, of course," Charlotte answered. "It *will* be
good to see Aunt Mary. I haven't seen her in ever
so long."

"She doesn't get away from Ransome Park
often, because of her rheumatism," Diana said.
"But I always send her news of you in my letters.
She will be so pleased to see how you have
grown up!"

Charlotte gave her a tentative smile. Lady Caroline laughed, her usual silvery trill, and said, "La,
my father says that when Lady Ransome was
young she cut quite a dash about Town! He told
me . . ."

And Caroline launched into a half-remembered,
gossipy tale of Lady Ransome at Ranelagh as a
young wife, amid much laughter and a few
shocked "No!"'s from Charlotte. Diana gave the
girls an indulgent smile, and turned her attention
to the passing scenery.

Not much had changed in this place since she
traveled here to stay with her Aunt Mary so many
years ago, a disgraced and heartbroken girl. It had
even been near this time of year, when the trees
were shedding their winter doldrums to clad
themselves in green, and birds were busily build-

ing nests in the hedgerows. The road to Ransome Park was a pretty one, full of the pastoral beauties so beloved of English poets. Then, she had been too miserable to notice anything beyond her own disappointment. Now, though, she took it all in, absorbed it into her very essence. She had been in Town too long. Perhaps lonely too long.

She reached up and touched the small lump of her golden locket, hidden beneath her plum wool travel gown.

The carriage slowed, and turned in the open wrought iron gates that led to the house. The driveway was not long but was wide, lined with more towering trees, more fenced paddocks where colts galloped and horses watched with careful eyes. As the house came into view, even Lady Caroline grew quiet, watching out the window as they drew ever closer.

Ransome Park was not an old dwelling. In fact, it had been built by Lady Ransome's late husband's father. But it had the appearance of being vastly ancient, its dark stone walls creeping with thick ivy, its windows mullioned. Carved gargoyles leered down from the rooftop.

"Lady Ransome's father-in-law was a great scholar of medieval history," Diana explained. "And when it proved impractical to actually dwell in a fourteenth-century keep, he built one for himself."

"Pooh!" Lady Caroline exclaimed. "I would wager there is even a dungeon. Shall we seek it out, Charlotte? Rattle some chains about in the middle of the night, things like that?"

Charlotte stared out at the house, biting her lower lip in uncertainty. "I'm not sure that's such a good idea, Caro. What if we woke ghosts that were already there? They would not be happy we usurped their place." A tiny smile quirked at the corner of her mouth, the only sign that she was joking.

Caroline laughed heartily, and leapt down from the carriage as soon as they rolled to a stop and the door opened. "If there *are* ghosts, we shall surely find them!"

"I have no doubt you will, Caro," Charlotte answered. She exited in a more sedate manner, taking the footman's hand as he helped her down to the drive.

Diana followed, clasping Charlotte's fingers reassuringly as they strolled toward the house. "If there *were* any ghosts at Ransome Park, I'm sure Aunt Mary chased them away long ago."

The front door burst open, and three tiny, madly yapping lapdogs came dashing down the steps, twining themselves around everyone's ankles like miniature whirlwinds. Miss Bourne, Aunt Mary's longtime companion, raced in their wake, struggling to scoop them up. They eluded her at every turn.

"Oh, Bon-Bon!" she cried, finally clasping one little black dog by its jeweled collar and catching it in her hands. "I am sorry, Lady Gilbert. Such a welcome for you! They are so very wild."

"Quite all right, Miss Bourne," Diana assured her, laughing. "At least we know we are expected."

"They're adorable!" Charlotte cooed, cradling a cream-colored puppy in her arms. Charlotte was never shy with animals or children.

Caroline dodged away from the tiny horde, brushing at her dark blue skirts as if they could not be besmirched by so much as one dog hair.

"Ah!" a voice cried from the top of the steps. "It is my lovely nieces, arrived at last."

Lady Ransome stood poised in the doorway, leaning on her stick. This, however, was her only sign of any infirmity. She was as tall and lovely as ever, with sparkling blue eyes and copious white curls spilling from beneath her lace cap.

"Aunt Mary!" Diana said, dashing up the steps to kiss Lady Ransome's offered cheek. It was soft, scented with rice powder. "What a delight to see you again."

"It has been far too long, my dear Di." Lady Ransome took her hands, her gaze scanning Diana's face as if seeking any sign of unhappiness she could soothe. Just as she had when Diana was a girl. "London life certainly seems to agree with you."

As country life with her husband had not? Diana just smiled and squeezed her aunt's hand. "It is very lively there, to be sure. I so enjoy the theater and the bookshops! But I'm glad to be able to spend some quiet time here with you."

"I hope we shan't be *too* quiet! Especially with these lovely young ladies in residence." Lady Ransome turned to Charlotte and Caroline, who left off their wrangles with the dogs to come and greet their hostess. Lady Ransome reached out to pat Charlotte's pale cheek. "This must be dear little Charlotte! How very grown-up you have become."

Diana shifted to stand beside her sister, in case shyness should overtake her. Charlotte, though, appeared perfectly at ease. The romp with the dogs had soothed her nerves, and she was once again happy. She gave her aunt a curtsy and a polite smile.

"How do you do, Lady Ransome?" Charlotte said softly.

"Now, now, none of that nonsense! I am Aunt Mary. And this must be your friend, the famous Lady Caroline?"

Caroline also curtsied, a wide smile deepening the dimples of her cheeks. "I'm very pleased to meet you, Lady Ransome. My parents send their compliments, and their thanks for your kind invitation to me."

Lady Ransome's lips pursed. "Your parents? Yes—certainly they would. Well, my dears, do come inside! You must be greatly fatigued after your long journey, and it is abominably rude of me to keep you standing about in the wind. Come inside and have some tea. Miss Bourne will see to the doggies."

So, leaving Miss Bourne to her travails with the "doggies," Diana followed her aunt through the immense, faux-baronial hall lined with swords, axes, and various bits of armor. The girls trailed behind her, their whispers echoing off the stone floors. There were stifled giggles, but Diana did not have the heart to admonish them. It *was* rather too much like something from a horrid novel, where evil knights lurked in the shadows waiting to ravish fair maidens. When Diana was a girl, influenced deeply by epic poems, she had reveled in the eeriness of the ancient armor, the mystery of dark corners.

Now, she wondered only if her maid had remembered to pack her furs.

The drawing room, fortunately, was of a more modern—and comfortable—design. The ceiling did not soar dozens of feet up to darkened beams; the fireplaces did not look ready to receive a spit boar. And there were no axes of any kind on the walls. Instead, the cozy space was painted a cheerful pale yellow, edged in bright white cornices. The furniture was all white wood and gilt, upholstered in soft green brocade and scattered with embroidered cushions. The walls were hung with a variety of portraits and pastoral landscapes, the faded green and yellow carpet scattered with chewed dog toys. A warm fire crackled in the white marble grate, as two maids laid out tea on a low table beside it.

"Now, we can settle in and have a nice chat, without all those rusting suits of armor peering at us," Lady Ransome said, seating herself in a tapestry-covered armchair. "Diana, would you be so kind as to pour for us? And tell me all the Town gossip. Is it true what I hear about poor Lady Glossop?"

As Diana poured out the tea and passed around plates of cakes and sandwiches (assisted by Miss

Bourne, who soon reappeared sans animals), they chatted of inconsequential things. The theater, marriages and births among their acquaintances, fashions, the doings of Lady Ransome's neighbors. When the last cake was consumed, the girls wandered away to examine a pianoforte in the corner, and Lady Ransome settled back again amid the cushions of her chair.

Diana could tell by the glint in her aunt's eye that she had not said all she intended to. Not by a mile.

"They are very pretty girls," Lady Ransome said. "We shall be much livelier here at Ransome Park now they have arrived."

Diana smiled at her over the rim of her teacup. "Lady Caroline is certainly very lively. I fear Charlotte is still a bit shy."

Lady Ransome waved her hand in a dismissive gesture. "What is shyness when a girl has beauty and sweetness—and a fine dowry. I assume she *is* well set up there?"

Diana was not even surprised at her aunt's bluntness. "Oh, yes. Our parents left her a tidy sum, and I have been able to add a bit from my own coffers. Not so much that she will be a prey to fortune hunters, but enough to be attractive to worthy young men."

Lady Ransome nodded approvingly. "Very

good. She seems a dear girl, and I should like to see her comfortable in life. Like yourself."

Diana just nodded placidly, her features long schooled into pleasant lines that gave away not a hint of any true emotion or thought. To the world at large it had *always* seemed she was "properly set up" in life. A titled husband, a fine townhouse, a secure place in Society. Lord Gilbert had not been a terrible husband. They had little in common, of course, but he was of an amiable disposition, and when he died he left her the house and an extremely generous annuity. No children, sadly, but she was free to pursue her own interests in life.

"I am very comfortable, yes," Diana said, setting her cup down neatly on the tea table.

"And happy with the Town life?"

"Quite happy. I am a member of several literary and philosophical societies, and go out in company almost every evening. There is always something interesting going on."

"Hm, yes. I felt the same when I was young. My life was full of social doings, though in my day London was far more rackety than it is now! These modern scandals are nothing compared to ours." Lady Ransome paused, her gaze falling on the girls, who were laughing over a piece of music. Miss Bourne placidly embroidered in the corner, taking no notice of any of them. "Gilbert was a good enough man, in his own way, and certainly cared about you."

"As I did him."

"Yes. You were an exemplary wife, Diana. But you can't fool me. I am an old lady, and I have seen everything in my time. There was no passion in your heart for your husband. And who could blame you? You were a sensitive girl, full of sensibility, and he thought of nothing but his guns and horses."

Diana looked away from her aunt, unable to meet that shrewd gaze any longer. "Were my feelings so very obvious, then?"

"Only to me. I know you well, you see—you were much like me when I was a girl, and a country sportsman with no adventure in his heart was not the best match for you. But you did your duty, my dear. And now you are free. What do you intend to do now?"

Diana blinked. "Do? Why—I will usher my sister through her Seasons, and hope she finds a more compatible mate. Then perhaps I will travel on the Continent for a while. I've always longed to see other lands."

"Yes. I remember all those novels you pored over as a girl. Italy is so fashionable these days, and I hear that Italian men are *beautiful*. And very accomplished in the boudoir."

"Aunt Mary!" Diana cried, feeling an embarrassing warmth flood her cheeks. Such a nuisance—she was a widow, not a schoolgirl to blush at every word! She glanced over at Charlotte and Caroline, but they were too far away to hear, and were occupied with themselves.

"What? Italian men don't appeal, my dear? Have any Englishmen caught your fancy since Gilbert popped off to his reward?"

An image flashed in Diana's mind, a memory of eyes like the sky and glossy black hair, of kisses that thrilled her to her youthful toes. She reached up and touched the hidden locket. "No, not since Gilbert died."

"That is too bad. Not a single man to catch your fancy in London, eh? Well, they can be a bloodless lot, compared to the men of my young days. Italy will be a different kettle of fish, though, mark my words. You are still young, Di, and very pretty. No need to bury yourself in the marble mausoleum yet."

Diana laughed. "It's hardly a question of entombment, Aunt Mary. I enjoy my life very much, and right now my attention is focused on finding a husband for Charlotte. Not a lover for myself."

45

"Who says you can't do two things at once? Charlotte is a pretty girl. You will have no difficulty in finding her a suitable *parti*." Lady Ransome ran a thoughtful touch over the polished handle of her stick. "Perhaps I can even help you with that."

Diana gave her aunt a suspicious glance. She did not quite trust that innocent tone. "Oh, yes?"

"I have invited a few young men to this party."

"What sort of young men?"

"Oh, I am sure you know them. Lord Edward Sutton, youngest son of the Duke of Conway, and his friend Mr. Roland Kirk-Bedwin. Lord Edward's parents are old friends of mine, and I have heard he is a most intellectual young man. And if Mr. Kirk-Bedwin is anything like his grandfather, he will have a very pleasing visage. Quite an ornament to our party."

Diana pressed her lips together. She *did* know the two young men. Lord Edward seemed a harmless sort, very well connected and wealthy, too preoccupied with intellectual matters to be a rake. She would have no objections if Charlotte took a liking to him. Mr. Kirk-Bedwin, on the other hand, *was* very handsome, and charming, too. But he was known to live rather high, and had no money of his own yet, only the prospect of being his rather Puritanical uncle's heir. All the young ladies swooned over him, and he had been in pursuit of Lady Caroline, a girl who matched him in dash and verve. Until she sensibly dropped him, and not even Charlotte knew why.

What was her aunt thinking? Lady Ransome might live in the country, but Diana knew very well she was entirely informed about Societal doings. She would know the history of Mr. Kirk-Bedwin's dealings with Lady Caroline. What was her game?

Yet Diana could see that her aunt would not give her hand away so early. Diana merely nodded, and said, "Yes. Very amiable young men."

"I have also asked one of my neighbors, a Mr. Frederick Parcival. An excellent card player, and he plays the pianoforte and reads poetry, just as you do, my dear. The neighborhood has been much livelier since he came to live at the Grange."

Diana gave her aunt a wry grin. "You needn't matchmake for *me*, Aunt Mary."

Lady Ransome opened her eyes wide in feigned innocence. "My dear! I would never presume. I just thought you might enjoy someone to talk of books with you. You are so accustomed to such things in Town."

"And so I will, I'm sure." Diana felt it best to turn the subject. "Who else will we see here at Ransome Park?"

"Oh, not a large party, though we will have to have a dance one evening, with more of the neighbors invited in. I have asked another new neighbor, Mrs. Elizabeth Damer, a young widow like yourself, though not as comfortable as you, I think. And my own friend, Mrs. Cole. She moved into Lilac Cottage last year, and we have quite become bosom bows. It's so pleasant to have someone my own age to talk with! She will be here tomorrow, along with her son."

Cole? Diana's hands tightened on the arms of her chair. A Mrs. Cole and her son, coming here to Ransome Park. Strange, how after so many years the very sound of the name was enough to give her a start.

It cannot be the same people, she told herself. *Cole is a common name.*

Tom Cole had gone off to North America years ago. No doubt he was still there, with a colonial wife and eight children, and he never thought of his youthful romance any longer. Unlike her own silly self.

"I look forward to meeting them," Diana murmured.

"I myself have not yet met Mr. Cole, but from what his mother says he is a most affectionate son, and very well set up in the world. My friend quite dotes on him. She says . . ." Lady Ransome suddenly broke off her words, a frown creasing her brow. "Why, Diana! Are you well? You look suddenly pale."

Diana gave her a weak smile. "I'm just tired. It was a long drive."

"Of course. What a ridiculous old woman I am, chattering away at you! You must rest before dinner. We will be very informal this evening. The rest of the guests won't arrive until tomorrow. Miss Bourne will show you to your room. It's the same one you used before."

"Thank you, Aunt Mary." Diana rose from her chair and went to kiss her aunt's cheek. "It *is* good to see you again."

Lady Ransome caught her hand in a tight clasp. "I can't tell you how glad I am you have come for a visit, Di. It gets rather lonely here sometimes, living in the country."

"It gets a bit lonely in Town, too." Diana gave her aunt one last smile, and turned to call out, "Charlotte, Lady Caroline, would you like to rest before dinner?"

"Of course, Di," Charlotte answered for them both, though Lady Caroline looked as if she could walk a mile and not be wearied. The three of them followed Miss Bourne back into the baronial hall and up the grand staircase.

At the doorway, Diana glanced back to see her

aunt watching after them, a distinctively wistful smile on her face.

Wistful was not a word she would ever have used to describe Lady Ransome. Diana was suddenly very glad indeed they had come to Ransome Park. Even if a family named Cole was soon to arrive.

Chapter Three

"*O*h, Tom. I simply don't know what clothes to take! What if the other guests are very grand? I should not want to disgrace myself, or you."

Tom Cole glanced up from his newspaper to smile at his mother, who sat across the table from him in the cheerful breakfast room of Lilac Cottage. She was still a very pretty woman, despite the long years in exile. Still small and slim, with hardly a thread of gray in her soft brown hair, and gentle blue eyes set off by her blue muslin morning gown. But her brow was furrowed in thought, her hand fluttering uncertainly before landing on her teacup. She raised it up, only to set it back down without taking a sip.

She *was* in a state. Tom almost regretted agreeing to go with her to this Lady Ransome's party if it cut up her peace like this. Rachel had been so happy since they returned from North America with their new fortune, and he bought her this fine country house. She took such joy in arranging the rooms to her liking, and restoring the neglected gardens to their old beauty. Flowers were her great delight, and she spent hours contentedly puttering in her plots and groves. He had been happy to hear she formed a friendship with Lady Ransome, for the two ladies seemed to have many interests in common, and his mother needed a female friend of her own age. There had been precious few in York.

Yet he *had* been wary of Lady Ransome's rank. He himself, in his new home in London, had no trouble forming acquaintances, though they were not of the first rank. His own circle was composed of wealthy merchants such as himself, men who had made their fortunes in trade and their wives who schemed to matchmake for him, despite his protests that he did not yet mean to wed. Men of the aristocracy were happy to lunch with him at times, happy to ask his advice on financial matters. *Their* wives—well, some of them were cool in the extreme when they happened to meet, which was not often. And some of them were quite the opposite, casting him speculative glances from beneath their feathered bonnets.

No—Tom had very little use for the so-called *ton*. He remembered all too well what people of rank had done to him when he was a young, foolishly romantic man. He had a sudden memory of large brown eyes gazing up at him adoringly, soft lips yielding beneath his own. He ruthlessly pushed the thought of *her* away, as he always did.

No wonder he was wary of aristocrats and their motives. But his mother did like Lady Ransome, and he hated to curtail any of her pleasures. She had had few enough in her life. He even agreed to go with her to this house party when she asked him to. Now he was not sure they should have accepted, if it put her into such anxiety.

He gave her a reassuring smile, and folded his paper and placed it next to his plate. "Your clothes are lovely, Mother. Did you not order them up especially from Madame Dupret when you last visited me in Town?"

"Oh, yes, dear, they are very smart to be sure. But what if they are—too smart?"

Too smart? Tom had to confess himself a bit bewildered by her feminine qualms. There had been very little time to worry about ribbons and furbelows in the snowy wilds of North America, where his main concern had been trapping enough mink and beaver before the next shipment to England left. It was rather a pleasant feeling, to know that he and his mother would never have to worry about such things again, that she could concern herself with clothes and parties. *That* was why he had worked so hard all this time.

Not for a girl with soft hands, a gentle smile, and privilege in the very air about her.

"Do you not wear your new gowns when you and Lady Ransome meet?" he asked.

"Oh, yes, certainly."

"And does she seem—disapproving?" If she did, then Tom would have something—several things—to say to the lady, countess or not. No one insulted his mother.

"Of course not. She is a very dear friend."

"Then you have nothing to worry about. You need only be concerned with enjoying yourself, and looking lovely, as you always do."

Rachel smiled at last, and took a sip of her tea. "I'm sure you're right, dear. I can be so silly sometimes."

"Not at all." Tom rose from the table and went around to kiss his mother's cheek. "I have to do some work in the library, and we will call for the carriage this afternoon to take us to Ransome Park."

"That sounds good, dear. Don't work too hard."
She suddenly reached out and caught his hand,
her eyes serious as she stared up at him. "This is
the time we should enjoy our lives. You've strug-
gled so much for all the good things you've
earned. Now you should have a home of your
own."

Her words were frighteningly close to his own
earlier thoughts, but he had always thought his
mother was not overly concerned about him. He
tried to always show her that he was content with
his life, and so he was—most of the time.

He just grinned at her, and said, "You are only
trying to gain grandchildren, Mother."

She laughed. "It is true that I would like a
grandchild or two to toddle about with me in the
garden. But I want your happiness the most."

"I am happy," he said.

"Are you? Truly?"

"Of course, Mother. Now, I really must get
some work done."

He left her to finish her breakfast, and went
down the corridor to his library. Though the
house was really his mother's, as he had purchased it for her use and visited only once in a
while, she insisted on setting aside the small library for him. Her own collection of popular horrid novels she kept in her private sitting room,

and she decorated the library in comfortable, masculine style, with deep chairs of burgundy velvet, mahogany display tables, a massive desk. Tom himself filled the shelves with his own volumes.

He studied them now, those shelves full of beautiful, leather-bound volumes, each one beloved. Books were rare in North America, cherished no matter what they were, and reading had always been a joy to him. When they returned to England, wealthy and comfortable at last, the first thing he did was place orders with booksellers.

He ran a callused fingertip over the worn spine of *Romeo and Juliet*, and remembered again Diana and her dark eyes, bright as the night stars. Strange that he should think of her twice in one day; it had been so long since he saw her last. She had loved poetry, too; they used to read Shakespeare together when they met secretly, her voice rising and falling dramatically with the musical words. He used to imagine he heard her voice again, on cold, lonely nights in exile, that she was beside him with her gentle smile and ardent kisses.

Over the years, her memory faded a bit, the remembered heart-shaped face growing blurred at the edges, the voice fainter. He never forgot her entirely, though. She had been his Juliet.

He pushed the volume to the back of the shelf,

and turned away from all the old memories. That was all long in the past, when he had been fool enough to believe in the emotions spoken of so eloquently in romantic poetry. *She* was long in the past, and was probably a stout Society matron by now, with six brats clinging to her and a bluff, country aristocrat husband.

Perhaps his mother was right. Perhaps it was time for him to set up a proper home of his own, to buy a townhouse and move out of his bachelor rooms. Time to offer for one of his friends' pretty daughters and give his mother grandchildren to dote on. A wife could only do him good in his business, if she was charming and sensible. And he himself was sometimes (dared he say it?) lonely.

But would this new wife like poetry?

Tom shook his head, and went to the desk to bring out the paperwork that awaited his attention. He could do nothing about any marital schemes until after this blasted house party, anyway. He might as well get some business done. That was the one thing he was confident of accomplishing to satisfaction—business.

Romance had never been his forte at all.

Chapter Four

*D*iana stood at her bedroom window at Ransome Park, sipping at her cup of chocolate and watching the morning light spread over the gardens. It was a lovely sight; Aunt Mary was especially proud of her gardens, and they were always creatively arranged and immaculately maintained. The pale yellow sun burned away the last of the predawn mist, revealing the tumbling array of red, yellow, and pink blossoms.

She was habitually an early riser, even in Town. There was something very appealing about the quiet, the solitude, the feeling that she was all alone and could be herself, even if only for a short hour or two. In Town, one had to wear so many masks. Here in the country, the morning was even more delicious. Soon enough, the other guests would arrive and she would have to take up one of her masks again. Just not quite yet.

As she took another drink of chocolate, she saw that she was not the only early riser. Charlotte and Lady Caroline strolled into view in the garden below, arm in arm. They were dressed simply in their plain muslin morning gowns, their hair hanging loose down their backs. Laughter reverberated up to Diana's ears, even through the window glass.

Diana smiled. When Charlotte first met Lady Caroline Reid in Hatchards and formed a friendship with her, Diana had not been sure that was such a good idea. Lady Caroline had a reputation for being very—lively. There was never any outright scandal in her behavior, nothing that any but the most high sticklers would snub her for. But there *was* gossip, especially when her expected betrothal to Roland Kirk-Bedwin was never announced.

Charlotte was a very different sort of person, quiet, country-raised, a bit shy. Diana was not sure that Lady Caroline would be the best friend for her, but the two seemed closer than ever now. Caroline had helped Charlotte come out of her shell, and perhaps Charlotte had helped Caroline to calm down a bit. There was always the chance Lady Caroline would become bored, of course, and move on to a new bosom bow, but for now they seemed most content in each other's company.

Diana felt the smallest pang of envy. It had been so very long since she had such a friend, someone to speak to honestly, to share her interests with freely. Her husband, though a good enough man, had not understood her love of books, her craving for artistic beauty.

She finished the last of her chocolate and turned away from the window. There was no time now for such maudlin thoughts! She was a fortunate woman, with independent means and a very interesting life. "Soul mates" were merely a devising of the poets; they did not exist in real life. She had believed in such things once, when she was a girl. No longer.

She had to bathe and dress, for there was much she could do to help her aunt before the guests arrived. It was sure to be an eventful party, at any rate, and she would have no time for sentimental memories.

No time at all.

Charlotte laughed helplessly at the wild story Caroline was telling her, a tale that somehow involved pigs in Green Park, and people they knew in Town. Caroline's hands gestured in the air as she illustrated a particularly colorful point, and she twirled around on the garden path until her red hair flew out in a banner.

"Oh, Caroline, what a wheeze!" Charlotte gasped. "How do you find yourself in such situations?"

Caroline grinned. "I know all the best people, of course! And so do you. Think of all the fun we will have again next Season."

Charlotte shook her head, and sat down on the nearest granite bench. She wasn't really sure that releasing a porcine herd into the park *did* sound like fun, though hearing about it certainly was. Surely there would be far too much noise and confusion. "Perhaps."

"There is no *perhaps* about it, Charlotte." Caroline swirled over to sit beside her on the bench. "I am so glad you and I have become friends. I feel like I can always be myself with you, not like with my family and everyone else. They all— expect so much. It is very wearying."

Charlotte peeked over at her. Caroline *did* appear more relaxed here at Ransome Park, not so very brittle and fragile. The hectic light was gone from her eyes. "Did Mr. Kirk-Bedwin—expect too much?" she asked carefully. Caroline did not like to speak of Roland Kirk-Bedwin at all. She always turned away at mention of him, changing the subject with a bright, loud laugh.

Charlotte did not understand why. She thought Mr. Kirk-Bedwin was quite handsome, with his tall figure and waving dark brown hair, his fashionable clothes and exquisite horses. If he were to look at *her*, Charlotte was sure she would faint away. But there was no fear of that. He had eyes and dances only for Caroline, and Charlotte was just a quiet country mouse. She would have to settle for another country squire, like her sister's late husband, because a dasher like Mr. Kirk-Bedwin would never look twice at her.

He seemed perfect for Caroline, which made her rejection of him even more mystifying.

Caroline did not change the subject this time, nor did she dive wholeheartedly into Charlotte's question. Caroline plucked at her skirt, staring down at the white muslin as if she saw something fascinating printed there. When she did speak, her tone was uncharacteristically serious.

"When Mr. Kirk-Bedwin first began to pay attention to me," she said quietly, "I was—well, rather flattered. Lady Emma Benton was *so* wild for him, you know. Every man in Town was in love with her, but he gave her no mind at all. She was always so very annoying, you see, with her gossips about me and her titters behind her fan at balls when she 'complimented' my gowns. I was happy to accept his attentions when I saw how angry it made her, and I do like him. He is wickedly funny! But . . .''

Her voice faded, and her skirt-plucking grew more agitated. Charlotte stared at her in amazement. Such things as scoring off another lady by encouraging a man's attentions just seemed—not right. Yet she knew Caroline had no real malice in her. It must have seemed a mere silly game, like the pigs in Green Park. Still, Charlotte had to confess herself baffled.

"Then what happened?" she gently prompted.

"Then suddenly it seemed not a game anymore," Caroline murmured, flattening her palm against her skirt. "There was talk that he meant to offer for me, that we were expected to marry."

"That surprised you?" Charlotte asked, still trying to work things out in her mind. Was marriage not the purpose of such flirtations, in the end?

"Yes! I thought we were just larking around a bit, having a wheeze. How could he want to marry me? We would be an utter disaster together! And besides that . . .''

"Besides what, Caro?"

Caroline glanced up, and Charlotte was shocked to see the sheen of tears in her eyes. Charlotte took her hand gently, and whispered, "Is there someone else you like more?"

Caroline gave a jerky nod. "I have been in love

with him all Season, but he would never think of me that way! I am not good enough for him, Charlotte.''

Caroline Reid, not good enough for someone? Why, she was a Toast, a Diamond! A great beauty. Not like Charlotte, and her dull, pale looks. Charlotte could not imagine any man Caroline couldn't have. "Of course you are 'good enough,' Caro! Whatever do you mean? Who could this man be? The King of Araby or something?''

Caroline gave her a sad smile, completely unlike her usual merry grins. "Dear, sweet Charlotte. How could you understand? You are an angel, fit for the very best of men. My love is hopeless. He is not for me.''

Charlotte still feared she did not understand, and she had a hundred questions for her friend. Who was this man? Why would he think Caroline was not good enough for him? How could Caroline just give up like that? But Caroline had obviously finished her confidences. She gave a bright smile and jumped to her feet, hurrying off down the pathway before Charlotte could even rise.

"Do you suppose breakfast is laid out yet?" Caroline called back over her shoulder. "I am utterly famished!''

Chapter Five

*D*iana stared at her reflection in the mirror, reaching up to adjust the high frill of her chemisette that concealed her little gold locket. The guests would begin arriving at any moment, and Aunt Mary would expect her to be on hand to help greet them. Diana had always prided herself on her ability to be dressed, all neat and tidy, ready for any occasion in less time than it took most ladies to powder their cheeks. When she married and abandoned the pastel frills of her girlhood, she developed a practical but attractive style, based on simple lines and sensible colors, that allowed her to choose her gowns quickly and be gone. Why should she fuss? She hardly aspired to be an arbiter of fashion.

Today, though, she felt distinctly—fussy. Or something very like that. She could hardly tell *what* it was she felt, it was so very unlike her. Her plum-colored afternoon gown was one of her favorites, a color that suited her dark hair and eyes and was always presentable. With her cream-colored chemisette and garnet earrings, she was quite ready for greeting any guests. Yet something seemed not right. It was almost as if the woman who stared back from the glass was not *her* at all, but a stranger.

An elderly stranger.

Diana twitched at her sleeve, tugging the flared cuffs over her wrists. When had those lines formed around her eyes, at the edges of her lips? When had that single thread of gray appeared in her hair? She reached up and plucked the offending strand from her neat coiffure, wincing a bit at the sting.

She had become an old matron when she was not paying attention, a widowed chaperone at twenty-eight. Yet inside—inside her young self, that girl who raced headlong into life and emotions without a thought for the consequences, was trapped. Starving.

Diana stared down at the silver thread between her fingers. It was the mention of this family named Cole that had done this to her. She had tried so hard for so long to forget that boy, that beautiful young man with his farmer's callused hands and his poet's soul who had captured her heart. And mostly she succeeded. She was a grown woman now, with no room for foolish sentiment and useless memories.

Sometimes, though, a thought would creep up on her. A remembrance of his voice or kiss that brought the past rushing back to her. This friend of Lady Ransome, this Mrs. Cole, could not be related to him. He was thousands of miles away over the sea. Yet the sound of the name had made her pause and think.

That was always her problem. She *thought* too much.

Diana cast aside the single white hair and reached up to pat her chignon back into place, pushing the garnet combs more securely into the dark, wavy tresses. This was not time for nostalgia. She had duties to perform for her aunt, and she had to look after Charlotte. Her sister had been alone with Lady Caroline too long this morning, and with two young men arriving soon the girls would have to be watched closely.

As she reached for her paisley shawl, she heard the first carriage of the day rattle down the drive. The guests were here.

*　　*　　*

Mrs. Elizabeth Damer stared up at the Gothic mansion as her hired carriage bounced to a halt at the foot of the front steps. She had heard tell of Ransome Park, of course. It was the largest house in the neighborhood, and so unusual in its mock Middle Ages aspect. Yet she had never been a *guest* here before, or even expected to be, despite her own bold invitations to Lady Ransome to dine. Elizabeth had always thought she could brazen her way through anything; one had to, when one was struggling to conceal one's true circumstances from the world. She felt a strange flutter of nervousness in her stomach, though, now that she was actually here.

Who else would arrive? What would they think of her? What had they heard of her?

Elizabeth smoothed the hem of her new pelisse and reached up to straighten her chip straw, beribboned hat on her carefully arranged golden hair. Would her clothes be quite all right? They were all the crack in Town, of course—she still owed the modiste for them. Perhaps Lady Ransome had different expectations here in the country, though. That venerable lady was always dressed in elaborate, old-fashioned silks in grays or purples or greens, very expensive but several years out of date. Since Elizabeth could no longer afford to be seen in London, parties such as this were her only hope and she wanted to do them right.

Her only hope to find a husband flush enough in the pockets to afford her, that is.

Elizabeth peered out of the window at the house one more time. Well, she was here now, and if her clothes were wrong there was nothing to be done about it at this point. She had to make the best of it.

She straightened her shoulders, displaying her much-admired bosom to its best advantage, and pasted a brilliant smile on her lips. The hired driver opened the door and reached in to assist her in alighting. As she stepped down to the drive, she was careful to show a tasteful length of silk-stockinged ankle below the ruffled hem of her gown. A lady never knew who might be watching, after all.

Alas, the only person who was watching was Mr. Frederick Parcival, who had just arrived on horseback and was grinning down at her.

Her smile did not falter, but her eyes narrowed as she gazed at him. She had met Mr. Parcival at a dinner at the vicarage when she first arrived in the neighborhood, and had gauged him for what he was the instant he bowed over her hand, lingering a moment longer than was necessary. He was a handsome, impecunious rascal, just as her late husband had been. He was fun to banter with a bit, but he could not help her.

She had a suspicion he could use a great deal of help himself.

"Good afternoon, Mrs. Damer," he called, swinging down from his horse and striding to her side. She had to admit, he *did* have a fine figure. Too bad he did not have a purse to match.

"Good afternoon, Mr. Parcival," she answered coolly. "A pleasure to see you here."

His grin widened, eyes sparkling. Yes—a rascal indeed. "Is it, Mrs. Damer? I pray so. I must say, it is a glorious prospect to look forward to sharing your company this weekend. Country events can be so deadly dull, but never with such a charming lady in the gathering."

By Jove, but the man would be spouting poetry to her eyelashes and the glorious sun of her hair next! Elizabeth nearly rolled her eyes, but she had to confess it was rather nice to be flattered by a good-looking man again. The country *could* be deadly dull, he was right about that.

"I'm sure all the gathering will be charming," she said primly. "How can it be otherwise in dear Lady Ransome's house? Shall we go inside, Mr. Parcival?"

His grin twitched at the edges, as if mocking

her politeness. "Certainly, Mrs. Damer. Please, do lead on."

Elizabeth started up the front steps, gathering her skirts neatly in one hand so as not to muss the ruffles. She was quite sure Mr. Parcival watched the sway of her backside as she walked, but she dared not glance back to be sure. It did make her smile, though. Secretly.

Too bad the effect was ruined by a horde of tiny, yapping dogs rushing at her and catching those ruffles in their sharp little teeth!

Lord Edward Sutton peered closer at a stone ornament on the corner of Ransome Park, wishing his spectacles were not packed away in his valise. The Middle Ages were his great passion, and even an imitation keep held great interest for him. This appeared to be a most authentic re-creation of a French thirteenth-century gargoyle, but it was rather hard to make out the more minute details. Edward leaned nearer, squinting at the edges.

"Hello!"

A sudden voice startled him, nearly causing him to poke his eye out on the stone. He caught his balance and straightened up hastily, rubbing at his cheek. He squinted, just making out the outline of a girl standing a few feet away. Her pale dress seemed to glow.

"Hello," he murmured uncertainly.

"Oh, Lord Edward, you're hurt!" she cried, and her skirts whispered delicately as she hurried toward him. "I am so very sorry. I did not mean to startle you."

Edward blinked at her as she came closer. She obviously knew *him*, and once she was beside him he saw it was Miss Charlotte Hillard, Lady Caroline Reid's friend. Of course she would be here already—he remembered now that she was Lady Ransome's niece.

He wondered suddenly if Lady Caroline was here now, too, and his pulse gave a strange leap at the thought. *How very curious.*

But he had no time to properly analyze this reaction. Miss Hillard had whipped out a handkerchief and was pressing it to his abraded cheek. It smelled pleasantly of lilac, and the scent tickled at his nose.

"Quite all right, Miss Hillard," he answered. "I should not have been peering so closely at the gargoyle."

"You mean the menacing-looking creature? I did wonder what it was. There are so many curious things here at Ransome Park. I often wish I could spend more time here so I could research the architecture properly."

"Indeed?" Edward eyed Miss Hillard with more

interest. She had always been so quiet when they met in Town, so very much in the lovely Lady Caroline's shadow. Perhaps she was really some sort of scholar. "You are quite right about the interest of the house, Miss Hillard. I have only just arrived, of course, but I can see that this wing is distinctly influenced by the French style, while the portico is Italian. Florentine. Not entirely accurate, of course, but a very reasonable facsimile."

"Truly?" She peered up at the stone wall, shading her eyes with her hand against the afternoon light. "I had not thought of it like that, but you are quite right. The windows are obviously Norman."

Edward stared at her. Really, she was very pretty, with the sunlight glinting on her pale hair, and her green eyes glowing with interest. And she even knew Norman from Florentine!

"You study medieval architecture, Miss Hillard?" he asked, suddenly wishing he was a bit more like Roland. Now *he* knew how to talk to young ladies! Edward always felt so very tongue-tied around them, so awkward and unsure, especially around beauties like Lady Caroline. He never knew what might interest them.

Miss Hillard, though, might be different. Not like the frightening Lady Caroline.

A faint blush stained Miss Hillard's cheeks, adding to her shy prettiness. "Oh, no, not *study*, though I do find the period to be of great interest, especially the reign of Richard the Lion-Hearted." She paused, glancing suddenly away as if timid. Edward knew the feeling well. "You know, Lord Edward, there is an account of the building of Ransome Park in the library, which might be of some interest to you."

"Indeed it would!" Edward paused, unsure. He took a deep breath, and plunged forward. "Perhaps—perhaps *you* would care to show it to me, Miss Hillard?"

She gave him a surprised glance, her pink lips parted. "Why—of course, Lord Edward. I would be happy to help you in the library, if I can. My aunt also possesses a very fine edition of . . ."

"Charlotte! You sly puss, there you are," a merry voice called. A voice Edward recognized as belonging to Lady Caroline. Miss Hillard stepped away from him, her gaze falling to the ground. Edward was suddenly overcome by disappointment. What had Miss Hillard been about to say? And did she still want to show him the library?

Lady Caroline stepped up to his side with a peal of bright laughter. Her rich French perfume drowned out the sweet scent of lilacs, even though he still held Miss Hillard's handkerchief in his hand. He carefully slid it inside his coat just as Lady Caroline took his arm.

"Charlotte is always so shy, trying to hide from guests," Lady Caroline said gaily. "And you are terrible to encourage her so, Lord Edward! Not that you are any better, of course, running away as soon as you arrive. We would not have known you were here if I did not happen to catch a glimpse of your carriage from the window."

"Is my aunt looking for me, Caro?" Miss Hillard asked. Her voice was low and strained again.

"I don't know, but tea is being laid out in the drawing room," Lady Caroline answered. "I am sure you must be parched after your journey, Lord Edward! And I must have you tell me all the latest news of Town, of course."

Lady Caroline steered him toward the front steps, chatting about *ton* gossip all the way, leaning lightly against his shoulder.

Miss Hillard trailed behind them quietly, and Edward wondered if he should draw her forward and ask her more about the library. He could not speak, though. He scarcely dared move. Lady Caroline had him caught securely in her spell.

Roland Kirk-Bedwin watched as Lady Caroline led his friend Edward into the house, holding on to his arm, chattering and smiling up at him brightly. Charlotte Hillard trailed after them, and Edward looked utterly bemused. As always.

Roland would have been bemused himself, if he had not been so angry.

He scowled at the sight of Caroline so cozy with Edward, only vaguely aware that the groom who had dashed up to take his horse fell back with the force of that anger. Roland threw himself from the saddle and tore his riding gloves from his hands. Women were a confounded mystery, and Caroline Reid was the worst of the lot! Only last month she had been smiling at *him* like that, and now she had turned her charm on to poor, hapless Edward. Who knew what random chap she would choose next.

It would not be such a bad thing if Roland did not feel like such a fool. Flirtations often died a natural death, especially ones with young ladies of good family. The attraction would wane and nothing stronger would arise to take its place, so the acquaintance would burn away. He had met ladies of Caroline Reid's ilk before, rather daring, beautiful girls who wanted to feel brave and dangerous, and thought he was just the man to help her do that. He had no qualms about indulging them a bit, dancing with them, taking them riding in the park, playing piquet with them. But he knew where to draw the line, where to pull away.

With Caroline Reid it had been—different. He could not explain why exactly. Nothing in his rather vast experience with the fairer sex could prepare him for the force of her. She was beautiful, yes, but so were many other women. She had a—a spirit that attracted him, something in her that echoed his own longings. Or so he had imagined. Obviously, he was very wrong, for she had entirely dropped him, started refusing his invitations and sending back his bouquets, and now she was flirting with Edward.

Women were the most confounded nuisances.

But he would not think of her any longer. He had already scared the groom with his temper—he could not afford to do the same with Lady Ransome and her guests. He had to be on the "suitable wife" hunt again.

Slapping his gloves against his thigh, he took a step toward the house, prepared to do his duty as a guest. He had not even reached the front steps when the door opened and Charlotte Hillard came out again. She hurried down the steps and around the corner, her slippers flashing beneath the hem of her gown. Now, Miss Hillard was usually the most sedate of young ladies, pretty enough certainly but not terribly noticeable, especially since she was so often with Lady Caroline. He was curious what she was doing in such a hurry.

Roland turned his path and followed her around the corner of the house. She stood near a rather fearsome gargoyle, her head bent as she searched for something on the ground. What could she have lost? A billet-doux? A love token of some sort? Mildly intrigued, Roland moved closer and called out, "Lost something, Miss Hillard?"

She spun around, her pale pink skirts whirling around her legs, her eyes wide. "Mr. Kirk-Bedwin! I did not see you there."

"I only just arrived. May I help you in your search?"

She looked back down at the grass. "I lost a handkerchief. So silly, of course, but it has such a pretty embroidery on it. I should hate to lose it."

Roland gave her a gentle smile. She really was very pretty, and sweet, once out of Lady Caroline's vivid shadow. "Of course not. Nice embroidery should never be lost. What color is it?"

"White, with purple lilacs. Thank you so much, Mr. Kirk-Bedwin. It is kind of you to help."

She sounded dismayingly surprised that he *would* stop and help. Did he really seem too ungentlemanly to her, then?

They searched for a few moments in silence, but it soon became apparent that there was no handkerchief there.

Charlotte straightened, pushing back a stray lock of blond hair. "It must have blown away in the wind," she said. "We should go in for tea. My sister will be wanting to know where I am."

Roland offered his arm to her. She hesitated for a moment, but finally slid her hand into the crook of his elbow and let him lead her back toward the front of the house.

"I fear it will seem rather dull to you here, Mr. Kirk-Bedwin," she said softly. "After Town, that is. No theater or grand balls."

"No Vauxhall or Gunter's?" he said with a smile. Somehow, Miss Hillard made him feel—different. More gentle, more careful. As if he wanted to match her in kindness and sweetness. As if he ever could. He had been corrupted long ago. He would never be good enough to be *her* friend. But surely that did not mean he could not simply enjoy being in her angelic presence. Could it?

She laughed. "I fear not. You just seem . . ." Her words faded, and she gave a helpless little shrug.

"More of a city person?"

"Well, yes."

"I suppose I am. Yet the country certainly has its own pleasures. Fresh air, room to gallop—strolling along with a pretty girl."

She gave a small smile, and a lovely little dimple appeared deep in her pale cheek. "Are you flattering me, Mr. Kirk-Bedwin?"

"Not at all, Miss Hillard. Merely being honest."

"Then I thank you for the compliment," she said. But she still looked most doubtful. "Tell me about the Everard ball two weeks ago. I was sorry to miss it."

He told her inconsequential details of that fete, the last of the Season, as they entered the house and she led him toward the drawing room. Who had been there, what they wore, who made a cake of themselves in the card room. She nodded and laughed at all the correct places, and surrendered him to her aunt, Lady Ransome, who sat in her throne by the fireplace.

He was rather sorry to see Miss Hillard go, his gaze following her as she moved away to take a cup of tea from her sister. And he scarcely noticed Lady Caroline Reid, chatting with Edward in a window seat.

Well, well, he thought, as Miss Hillard smiled at him. Perhaps life was looking up.

Chapter Six

*D*iana stood behind her aunt's chair, sipping
at her tea and watching the gathered company. Charlotte and Lady Caroline's choices of
conversation partners were—curious. Lady Caroline sat in a window seat with the scholarly Lord
Edward Sutton, and Charlotte, after helping Diana
pour the tea, was happily chatting with Roland
Kirk-Bedwin, of all people. A handsome young
man, to be sure, but just the sort of person Charlotte always seemed most shy around—handsome,
charmingly teasing with the ladies, socially assured, yet always liable to land in the soup at any
moment. He did not look archly flirtatious now.
He listened to Charlotte with an intent, almost
bemused expression on his chiseled features.

How very odd, thought Diana, taking a slow sip.

He was not the sort of friend Charlotte needed, but surely it could not hurt for them just to talk together. Diana would keep a careful watch on them.

Just as her aunt was. Lady Ransome gossiped with Mrs. Damer, a flashily pretty young widow dressed in the very first stare of London fashion, yet her gaze often landed on the young couples with a speculative gleam. As if this was a scene in a play laid out just for her, and themselves all actors whose actions she was mildly curious about.

And, of course, that *was* what they were in many respects, summoned to Ransome Park because her aunt was bored and wished for a change. Diana had no trouble with amusing her aunt, if she could. Lady Ransome had been kind to her when she most needed a friend. Her only fear was that the doings of a respectable widow would not be enough.

"Another riveting day in the country, Lady Gilbert," a deep voice murmured in her ear, interrupting her musings. She frowned, and glanced over her shoulder to find Mr. Frederick Parcival grinning at her. He was apparently another neighbor of her aunt's, the gentleman who was 'good at cards.' He seemed to amuse Lady Ransome, but Diana had encountered his sort all too often in

Town. He was what Roland Kirk-Bedwin would be in another ten or fifteen years, if that young man did not find a reason to mend his ways soon. Handsome still, but fading, dissipated, almost desperate.

"It appears to be a pleasant prospect," she answered carefully.

"Oh, come now, Lady Gilbert," he said, still smirking. "You cannot tell me you prefer this ill-assorted group to a grand London rout, full of variety and interest."

"There is amusement and variety to be found wherever one goes," Diana said, losing patience. She was trying to keep an eye on her sister, and make certain her aunt had no need of her. She had no time to converse with this man, who was probably something of a fortune hunter. "If one has the wit to look for it."

"As I am sure you do, Lady Gilbert," Mr. Parcival said, obviously not fazed. "I believe I saw you once in Town, at a musical evening given by Lady Uckley. You were talking with old Mrs. Fielding, so obviously you *do* find interest wherever you go."

Diana vaguely recalled that evening. She had gone because a performance by a well-known Italian soprano was promised, but first they had to sit through an egregious harp program by Miss

Uckley. Not to mention conversing with deaf Mrs. Fielding. Not that she would admit that to Mr. Parcival.

"I do appreciate music, whenever I am given the opportunity to listen," she said.

"I am sure," he answered. "But I particularly remember that evening because you, Lady Gilbert, wore the most exquisite green satin gown, which made your hair glow like an autumn fire . . ."

Diana's lips tightened at this most improper comment, yet she had no time to snap back a down-putting reply. The drawing room door opened to admit some late arrivals, and Lady Ransome called out happily, "Mrs. Cole! Here at last. And this must be your handsome son."

Diana turned away from Mr. Parcival in relief to greet her aunt's friends. Only to freeze in mid-motion, her skin turning to tingling cold despite the warmth of the fire. A strange ringing vibrated in her ears. Her teacup rattled in its saucer, and she clutched at it with both hands to keep it from spilling.

The man who stood in the doorway, a small, slim older lady on his arm, a polite smile curving his lips, was Tom Cole. *Her* Tom Cole!

Diana shivered, and handed a passing footman her cup so she could clutch at the back of her aunt's chair and thus not fall to the floor. Her knees were shaking, and suddenly she was a love-struck girl again, filled with wild excitement, joyous need. She brushed her hand over her eyes, wondering if she was imagining things. No—it *was* him. Tom.

Older, of course, as was she. The boy she loved had been slender, wiry, his black hair overly long, curling over his collar and swooping carelessly along his brow. He had been sun-browned from working on his farm, but casually elegant, beautiful to her besotted eyes.

This man—and he was undoubtedly a man, not a youth—was still very handsome, but not in the cultured, careful way of Mr. Parcival. He was tall, broad-shouldered beneath his simple, well-cut wool coat, his skin bronzed and etched by harsh weather. His eyes were even more vividly blue in contrast, but where once they had glittered with enthusiasm and joyous, youthful love, now they were shuttered behind wariness and a certain glint of wry cynicism.

He observed the gathered company much as she had, as if watching a theatrical presentation. There was no joy there, though; it was as if he considered them a farce.

As well he might. A genteel company gathered

at tea, chatting and laughing, all real emotions and motives hidden beneath smiles and gossip must seem all too ridiculous after years abroad.

How long had he been back in England? What had happened to him over all this time? Had he thought of her, ever missed her? And—was he married now?

Diana's glance flickered past him to the doorway, which was now empty. No beautiful young lady followed, a shiny wedding band on her finger.

Diana felt so very warm suddenly, dizzy. As if she might faint, which she never had in her life. She held on to the back of the chair until her knuckles turned white. She had to take in a deep breath, careful breath, before she looked back to Tom Cole.

His own gaze was sliding over the room, moving ever closer to where she stood. *Blast!* She could not let him see her, not now, not when she was so flustered. She took a step back, toward the shadows at the edge of the room. If she could just avoid him, until this evening, perhaps, when she was more composed, more herself . . .

It was too late for that. Diana's aunt turned toward her and called, "Diana, my dear! Do come and meet my friend Mrs. Cole."

Diana smoothed her trembling hands over her

skirt before folding them neatly at her waist, trying to still their shaking. She smiled in her most practiced social fashion, but it felt like a painful grimace. Her knees were shaking, her mouth was dry. Yet she would not—*not!*—let them see that.

Mrs. Cole, who was still as pretty and kindly looking as all those years ago, gave a puzzled little frown, as if she felt she should know Diana and could not quite place her. When Diana looked at Tom, she saw his gorgeous blue eyes narrow, his shoulders stiffen.

"I have already met the Coles, Aunt Mary," she answered. Her voice was quiet, perhaps a bit rough, yet steady enough. *Thankfully.* "I am sure they will not remember, though. It was when I was a girl. How lovely to see you again, Mrs. Cole. Mr. Cole. You are both looking very well."

Mrs. Cole's puzzlement suddenly cleared, and a rush of bright color flooded her cheeks. She glanced uncertainly up at her son. "Oh—yes," she whispered. "Miss Hillard, is it not? I almost did not recognize you. I did not know you were Lady Ransome's niece."

Aunt Mary's lips dipped down at the corners, as if she knew something odd was afoot but could not tell what it was. Diana felt Tom's blue-flame gaze burning and intense on her skin, so she focused all her attention on Mrs. Cole and her aunt.

If she looked at him, she feared she might start laughing uncontrollably in hysteria—or crying at what was long lost.

"My niece is Lady Gilbert now," Lady Ransome said. "Though, sadly, she lost her husband last year. Come, my dear Mrs. Cole, I will introduce you to my other niece, Miss Charlotte Hillard. Perhaps you remember her, too?"

Lady Ransome rose from her chair, taking Mrs. Cole by the arm and leading her away, toward where Charlotte sat with Mr. Kirk-Bedwin. Mrs. Cole glanced back at her son, though there was no evading the will of Lady Ransome.

Diana was alone with Tom—or as alone as two people could be in a crowded drawing room. To her, it felt like they were an island of past regrets, marooned in a sad sea.

She felt him take a step closer to her, felt the heat from his body, his clean scent of soap and wool and leather. It reached out and wrapped around her. She swayed on her feet, overcome by the presence of *him*, before she could catch herself.

"You are looking well, Lady Gilbert," he murmured. His voice was as she remembered, so rich and deep, just as when he would read poetry to her. Now there was a sharp edge to it she had never heard before.

"As are you, Mr. Cole," she replied. She stared

straight ahead, at the simple knot of his stark white cravat. "It has been a very long time."

"Indeed it has."

There was so much more to say. Too much. Diana hardly knew where to start, or even if she *should* start. Some things were meant to remain in the past forever.

She also turned toward her sister, desperately seeking rescue. "You remember my sister Charlotte?"

"She was just a child when I left England," he answered.

"Of course. Come, I will introduce you to her. And to our other guests."

"That would be most pleasant," he said, painfully neutral.

They moved to the other groups, together yet so very far apart. Once she was immersed in the familiar social niceties, Diana was able to calm her shaking, to remember the truths of her everyday existence.

Soon, though, very soon, there would have to be a reckoning. What would happen to her careful world then?

Chapter Seven

*T*om studied the woman who stood beside him, conversing so politely with the people around them, a cool smile on her perfect pink lips. He had thought, after so many years in the wilderness, everything he had seen and done, that he could not be surprised by anything again.

He had been wrong.

Surprise was surely the least of his emotions when he saw the woman who walked toward him from the shadows. He knew her as soon as he saw her, despite the somber clothes and subdued hairstyle, despite the new dignity, the careful self-possession his childhood love had so adorably lacked. Her dark, gold-edged eyes—they were the same, so full of hidden depths, secrets he once longed to discover.

That spark was quickly covered, though, eclipsed by politeness and artifice. She looked like her mother in that instant, a cool aristocrat who kept a distance from the world around her.

His heart gave a pang for the lost girl, the girl with her hair waving down her back who would dash along the wooded path into his waiting arms, laughing as he swung her into the air. The girl he lost when he was sent away.

That pang, that flash of longing, was buried under a cynical thought. She seemed happy in her chosen life, in being Lady Gilbert, the condescending grande dame. Could she even remember what they once had in their youthful love?

Perhaps she did, for her cheeks turned pale when she saw him, and she trembled a bit beneath her stylish clothes. Or perhaps she just feared *he* remembered, and would reveal her secret.

He never would. Not necessarily for her sake, though he would never want to disoblige a lady if he could help it. More for the sake of what they once had, which was far too innocent and precious to allow people like this to snicker over.

People like the lady he was being introduced to now, a Mrs. Damer. She eyed him over the rim of her teacup, a distinctly feline smile on her lips. She was definitely a pretty woman, with too-bright golden hair arranged softly around her oval face, and green, almond-shaped eyes slightly tilted at the corners. She wore a yellow muslin gown with long, tight sleeves and a ribbon-edged bodice that hugged the curves of her generous bosom. A bosom she pressed against his arm every chance she had. Her laughter chimed like tiny silver bells in his ear.

Yes, a pretty woman, and one obviously practiced in flirtation. He could look at her and appreciate her charms, as one would a painting or a sculpture, yet somehow she left him feeling— detached. There was something in her gaze that reminded him too much of the women he had met so often in York, widows or young single ladies sent out to the colonies to find a husband. They had possessed just such an air of hard desperation, of calculation.

Tom had no inclination to be marched down the aisle in order to be someone's convenient open purse. So, he talked with Mrs. Damer, laughed with her, yet all the time his true attention was focused on Diana. She had drifted away from him to chat with a young, redheaded lady and a bespectacled gentleman. Her smile with them was gentle, her words too soft to overhear. As she listened, her head tilted to one side, as it once had when he read poetry to her.

Mrs. Damer's hand alighted on his arm, like a

fluttering little bird, and he suddenly longed to escape. To stand beside Diana and listen to her soft voice, to try to find his wild, romantic girl under the dignified lady. If she still existed at all, which he very much doubted. English Society had such a way of bearing down on people who dared to be different.

He *was* drawn away from Mrs. Damer, but not by Diana. "Mr. Cole," Lady Ransome said in her imperious voice. "Do please join us for a moment. Your mother has been telling me all sorts of fascinating tales of your life in North America. I would so love to hear of your own adventures in the wilderness. It must have been terrifically exciting."

Tom gave Lady Ransome a smile, and, murmuring his excuses to Mrs. Damer, moved away to sit by Lady Ransome and his mother. Mrs. Damer stared after him for a moment, and he could feel the force of her pout even from a distance. Fortunately, she soon turned away to talk with another man, a Mr. Parcival.

"I am not certain how *exciting* it was, Lady Ransome," he said. "Mostly it was cold and wet, a great deal of sitting around in the snow."

"Thomas, you are being too modest!" his mother chided. "Why, I was terrified every time he went on an expedition, Mary. The tales I would hear would keep me awake at night fretting over his safety."

Lady Ransome's eyebrows arched. Nearby, Tom sensed Diana's head turn in their direction, felt her gaze on him.

"Indeed?" Lady Ransome said. "It sounds like an adventure in a novel. I would so love to hear more."

"Tell her about the time a bear invaded your campsite," his mother urged. Despite her protestations about being kept awake at night by worries (which was probably true—his mother was quite a fretter), she never tired of begging for tales.

Tom did not like to talk about his time in the wilderness, seeking his fortune. What he said to Lady Ransome was fact—it was mostly cold and dull, setting traps and waiting for them to be sprung, endless travel from station to station. Few people to encounter, save for trappers and speculators and their quiet, native "wives." It was mostly a day-to-day battle against the elements, against boredom, against his own thoughts and memories that would creep up to haunt him on long, bone-chilling nights. It was a hard struggle, one that eventually paid off very handsomely, but not one he wanted to talk about. He wasn't even sure he *could* talk about it.

Yet his mother and Lady Ransome, and now

Mrs. Damer and Mr. Parcival, as well as Miss Hillard and Mr. Kirk-Bedwin, were watching him expectantly. They wanted to hear a tale of something different from their soft lives, he could tell from their eager expressions. Even Diana edged closer to their little group, and he suddenly wished he *did* have an exciting tale to tell, even if only for her, to see her eyes light up again as they once had.

The bear story would have to suffice. It was not a particularly thrilling tale; bears were a regular sight in the wilderness, and a man had to know how to evade them if he was to survive. If he could trap the creature, even better. The tale would be finer if he had, oh, perhaps fought the bear and killed him with his bare hands. But not even for Diana could he embellish like that. It was beyond his literary powers.

"It was two years ago, in the springtime," he began. "I had gone off on an expedition. . . ."

Diana watched Tom as he told his story, an account of a world so very alien to her own, a world he had lived in ever since they parted. An existence of snow and ice, of rough isolation, of people who shunned rules and lived in their own way, as she had never been brave enough to do.

She listened as he spoke of primeval woods

filled with dangerous creatures and perils at every turn, of harsh natural forces that cared nothing for human life or endeavors. He told it with an edge of careless laughter, as if facing down hungry bears was something everyone did from time to time, but Diana still shivered. He could have been *killed* in those woods. And she would never have seen him again, never even known what happened to him.

Not that she had ever really imagined she *would* see him again. Tom had become a cherished memory to her, but the solid remembrance of his warm presence had faded over time, and he had become to her a youthful folly. Now, seeing him again, watching his brilliant blue eyes flash as he talked, it became an agony to think of never seeing him again.

She suddenly wanted to cry, her eyes prickling at the sudden force of tears. She had been such a fool. She was *still* a fool.

Diana half-turned away from the raptly listening group, pressing her fingers to her eyes, willing the tears away. She was a grown woman now, a woman with a position and responsibilities, not an impulsive girl. She had to think of her reputation, of her sister.

She could *not* throw herself on her knees before him and beg him to carry her off to live in that wilderness with him, as she should have done all those years ago.

She drew in a deep breath, and slowly felt her control coming back to her. There would be time for tears later, perhaps, in the shelter of her own room. Tears and regrets. Not now. She could never let these people, especially Tom, see how she really felt.

Diana turned back around, only to find Tom's gaze on her as he spoke. He watched her steadily, his eyes unreadable. Once, he had known her so well. Could read her emotions with only a glance and a smile.

Se gave him her own flicker of a smile, and he returned a very small nod. *Later*, it seemed to say. *Later*.

Chapter Eight

*C*harlotte slowly ran the ivory-backed brush through her hair, staring out her bedroom window at the gathering dusk. She had always liked this time of day the best, when the rush of the afternoon was behind her and the swirl of the evening yet to begin. She could be quiet, just be herself with nothing expected of her. She could watch the sun sink in a fiery glow below the horizon, the tiny diamonds of the stars blink on one by one, and know that she was one day closer to the end of the Season. One day closer to freedom of a sort.

Actually, she never wanted these few precious moments to end. Never wanted to put on her gown and jewels and go to a crowded rout where she never knew what to say to people. But tonight she felt a strange restlessness. She wanted to do *something*, yet she did not know what. Run, dance, yell.

It was very unlike her.

She twisted the end of a strand of hair around her finger, remembering Mr. Kirk-Bedwin. She had noticed him in Town, of course. It was hard not to when he and Caroline were together. And Charlotte had always thought him handsome, but in that way that always made her feel nervous and flustered around men who possessed such beauty. She rarely spoke to Mr. Kirk-Bedwin, and when she did she felt all warm and flushed.

Today, when he approached her in the garden, it seemed—different. She *could* talk to him, and when he looked at her it was as if he saw her. Her, Charlotte, not Caroline's friend. And then he sat with her in the drawing room. It was, well, nice. Very nice. He was very interesting, with a caustic wit she could respond to.

Probably he was just trying to get close to Caroline again. Charlotte wasn't silly enough to think he had suddenly transferred his attentions from the Diamond of the Season to a wall mouse. Yet she did enjoy talking to him. After a time, she did not even feel shy anymore. They just conversed like two ordinary people, and she almost forgot how good-looking he was.

Almost.

Charlotte laughed aloud, and shrugged the heavy curtain of her hair back over her shoulder. It had been nice to feel easy in a man's company, even if only for a few minutes. She would just have to enjoy Mr. Kirk-Bedwin's attentions while she could. They would be gone soon enough, and she would have to find a nice, quiet, not too handsome young man to marry. Someone a bit like Lord Edward Sutton, perhaps.

An impatient knock sounded at the door. "Come in," Charlotte called, turning away from the gathering night.

Caroline burst in, scandalously clad in her chemise, two dinner gowns draped over her arm. Her red hair hung in a fiery rope down her back. "Oh, Charlotte! I need your help most desperately."

Charlotte giggled, and clapped her hand to her lips. "Caro! Whatever are you thinking? You can't run about dressed like that."

Caroline waved her hand in a careless gesture. "Oh, pooh! No one is about. They're all dressing for dinner. And I cannot decide which gown to wear!"

Charlotte turned back to the window to draw the draperies closed. As she grasped the edge of the slippery satin, she glimpsed a flicker of movement in the garden below, a tiny flash of hot red light. She peered closer, and saw that one person at least was not in his own room. Roland Kirk-Bedwin sat on a granite bench, smoking a thin cheroot. He seemed so solitary there, sitting in the darkness of the lonely evening.

The brief flare of red light lit up his face with a diabolical glow, and his expression, usually full of cynical laughter, was still and serious. What was he thinking? Charlotte suddenly longed to know, longed to run downstairs and sit beside him, be close to him.

Unconsciously, she raised her hand to touch the cool glass. His own hand lifted, and waved to her in greeting.

He had been watching *her*!

Charlotte jerked the draperies shut and clenched her fist in the soft fabric, suddenly warm even though the evening was cool. How long had he been sitting there, watching her brush her hair, watching her clad in her dressing gown?

"Charlotte? Is something wrong? You look all pink," Caroline said. She walked up to Charlotte's side and reached for the drapery, as if to draw it aside. Charlotte spun around, catching Caroline's arm and carrying her along back into the room.

"Not at all," Charlotte said, trying to laugh. "I've just been staring out at the sunset too long, I suppose, and it has given me a headache."

A tiny frown puckered between Caroline's eyes. "But it's been dark for ever so long."

Charlotte just shrugged, and drew Caroline over to sit on the settee. "Never mind that. You wanted to ask me something?"

Caroline smiled, appropriately distracted, and spread the two gowns over her lap. "I just wanted to see which of these frocks you thought the prettiest. I cannot decide."

Charlotte glanced down to see that one was a rose-pink gauze tunic over white silk, the other pale green muslin. Beyond that, she simply could not concentrate. She kept seeing Roland Kirk-Bedwin sitting outside, his hair tousled in the wind, watching her.

She gave her head a sharp shake and reached out to touch the edge of a pink flounce. "They are both lovely."

Caroline rattled the gauze impatiently. "But which is best?"

"The green, I suppose," Charlotte answered, just for something to reply.

That seemed to satisfy Caroline, who sat back with a sigh. "Then I will wear the green." She fiddled idly with a puffed sleeve of the chosen dress. Too idly. Charlotte suddenly had the suspicion that a fashion quandary was not what had sent Caroline dashing through the corridor in her undergarments.

Charlotte sat back against her own cushions and waited quietly. Waiting quietly was what she did best.

"Do you not think Lord Edward is handsome?" Caroline said lightly, smoothing down the green muslin sleeve.

Charlotte blinked. *Lord Edward?* "Why—I don't know. I suppose so. He certainly isn't hideous."

"No. I vow I never really noticed him until a few weeks ago, and today he just seemed so . . ." Caroline shook her head. "He seems very pleasant."

Charlotte had noticed Caroline conversing with Lord Edward for so long, of course. Yet she had thought perhaps it was merely a ploy to make Mr. Kirk-Bedwin jealous or some such nonsense. Lord Edward *was* a nice gentleman, Charlotte had always thought so, especially after meeting him examining the gargoyle today. He did not seem much Caroline's sort, though, despite his wealth and his ducal family.

But could—was it possible?—could Lord Edward be the man Caroline had spoken of in the garden?

"Caro," she said carefully. "Are you—interested in Lord Edward?"

Caroline laughed, but it was not her usual merry giggle. "Oh, pooh, no! He is so very serious and scholarly. I'm sure my rackety ways would bore him in a minute. I just never realized before that he has such nice eyes."

Nice eyes. Charlotte nodded slowly in agreement, though it was not Lord Edward's bespectacled orbs she saw in her mind. It was Roland Kirk-Bedwin's sherry-gold gaze, flashing with hidden laughter as he gazed down at her.

She swallowed hard past the lump in her throat. "But you talked with him for a very long time this afternoon, and he did not appear to be bored at all."

"That was only for an hour! Of course he could bear my company for that long. But he will probably be running away from me by the end of the party." Caroline kicked out her slippered foot, stirring the flounced hem of her chemise. "You seem just the sort of lady Lord Edward would admire, Charlotte."

"Me?" Charlotte cried, her voice high-pitched with surprise. She swallowed hard again, and repeated in a more modulated tone, "Me?"

"Yes, you. You're always reading and studying things. I'm sure you would—understand him."

Charlotte was thoroughly puzzled. "Do you want to understand Lord Edward?"

Caroline laughed again, still that strange,

strained chuckle. "Oh, no, of course not! I am just being silly. Now, I must go get dressed, and so should you, or we will be too late for dinner."

Caroline jumped up and bustled out of the room, taking her gowns with her and leaving Charlotte bewildered.

Who could Caroline really like now? And, more confusing, who did Charlotte like? There was a reason why some girls were not meant to be flirts. It was all far too complicated.

Roland sat on his cold stone bench for a long time after Charlotte Hillard jerked her draperies closed, staring up at the thin line of light showing through the glass. He had not come out here to spy on her; he didn't know that window above his seat was hers until she appeared there as twilight set in. He was just looking for a quiet spot to sit and enjoy a smoke, to think things out a bit.

Then Charlotte Hillard came to her window, her pale hair loose over her shoulders, clad in a simple white dressing gown. Her expression seemed so very far away, so full of dreams. He longed to know what it was she thought of so intently, what her daydreams were. She ran a brush slowly through her hair, letting the silvery strands float free in a halo around her face, and he knew her thoughts must be equally angelic.

Roland had never wanted to be good, never wanted to turn his actions to a higher plane, as his purse-string-holding uncle always urged him to do. Low actions were always so much more—pleasing. But at that moment, as he stared raptly up at the glowing vision of Charlotte Hillard, he wished he *could* be better, even if only for a moment. Only for her.

He wanted to kneel at her feet, to kiss her cool hands, and beg her to show him how to be better.

Then she saw him. For an instant, he could have sworn a flicker of longing passed over her own face. Or perhaps that was merely his own wishful thinking, for in the next second she yanked the draperies closed and he was alone in the darkness again.

Roland crushed the end of his cheroot under his boot and closed his eyes, inhaling the last of the sweet smoke on the night air. Charlotte Hillard was far too good for the likes of him. Even if he dared to get close to her, even if by some miracle she let him, the widowed sister who watched Miss Hillard with dragon eyes would chase him away.

Caroline Reid was much more his speed. Her beauty and fortune could be his salvation, and they could happily go on in their separate pleasures for a lifetime. Why, then, did the thought of

Lady Caroline now leave him with the cold sense of ashes in his heart?

He stood up to leave his bench, to go inside and dress for dinner, when the sharp crack of a footstep on the gravel pathway gave him pause. He glanced over his shoulder, half-expecting—or hoping—to see his angel in white. That was a foolish fancy, of course. She was safe behind her closed curtains, far away from the likes of him.

It was Edward who strolled up behind him, the rising moonlight glinting on his spectacles, a notebook tucked beneath his arm. His gaze was on the ground, an intent frown etched across his face.

"You're out late, old man," Roland called.

Edward started, and pushed his spectacles up on his nose as he squinted through the darkness. "Roland. I could say the same about you. I was just studying the Gothic ruin down at the edge of the garden. I daresay architecture isn't what is keeping *you* here, though."

"Hardly. I just wanted to have a quiet smoke."

"Of course."

They turned toward the house, making their leisurely way toward the terrace and the half-open glass doors. "Pleasant party," Roland commented idly.

"Yes, it is. Much more so than I thought it would be."

There was an odd note of bemusement in Edward's voice. Roland glanced over to find his friend gazing up at the house as if he had never quite seen it before, despite his minute study of the architectural details. Or perhaps it was the inhabitants of the house that had him so bemused.

Roland could understand that feeling.

"I saw you talking to Lady Caroline for a long time over tea," Roland said.

"Oh!" Edward gave another start, this one distinctly guilty, and his gaze shifted away. *What was this all about, then?* "Yes, I suppose I did converse with her for a while. She is a very interesting young lady."

Interesting? Roland tried to fathom what the two of them would have to talk about, but he had no idea. Edward was all books and ideas, Lady Caroline all parties and fast horses.

Hmm.

"What did you talk about?" he asked.

"Various matters," Edward answered. "She did not know a great deal about the history of Ransome Park, and she asked me questions about it. And we talked of ancient Greek drama and temple architecture."

Now *Roland* was the one who gave a start. He stared at Edward in astonishment. "Greek drama and temples?"

"Yes. It seems Lady Caroline has made quite a study of the Golden Age playwrights, such as Euripides. I know little about them myself, of course, since my area of interest is the Middle Ages, but she made some fascinating observations on the changing styles of that period as a whole."

"Lady Caroline did? Are you sure?"

Edward's frown deepened. "I do know who I was talking to, Roland. I am not so absentminded as all that. Of course it was Lady Caroline."

Edward went up the steps into the house, leaving Roland gazing after him. Well, well—would wonders never cease?

Chapter Nine

*T*om stopped at his mother's suite to fetch her before dinner. Despite the fact that she was among friends here, she still felt shy about going into parties alone. She was not yet quite ready, so he sat by the fireplace in her small sitting room to wait. Well, small was relative—the room was the size of their entire dwelling when they first arrived in North America.

Tom smiled at the memory, at the thought of how far they had come from those uncertain days. He sat back in a brocade armchair and reached for a book on the nearest table. Though he idly leafed through the pages, he did not really see the poems printed there. He could not turn his thoughts away from Diana Hillard.

No, not Diana Hillard now—Lady Gilbert.

He closed his eyes, and in his mind he saw her as she listened to his tales, her dark eyes wide, hands clenched, lips parted as she waited to see what would happen next. For a moment, she was no longer the aristocratic, somber widow. She was the girl he had once kissed and loved in secret, all full of the breathless joy of new life.

It had made him feel young again, too, before all the betrayals, the hardships of life in the colonies infected his life. But only for a moment. Then his story ended, and she stepped back, that mask once again falling into place over her beautiful face.

Tom closed the book, turning it over in his hands as he stared into the fire. Those days were long gone. He had to look to the future now, his own and his mother's. She had worked so very hard in North America. She deserved the finest life possible now.

Lady Ransome was a good friend to his mother, a very attentive neighbor, and it had been kind of her to invite them here for this party. But still his mother should have more. He could give her material luxuries, yet he could not give her one thing he knew she secretly longed for—a place in real Society.

He saw how avidly she read the papers in the morning, reveling in the gossip, searching out the most juicy tidbits. She knew all the doings of the *ton*, and he knew she would be thrilled beyond all words to have a place among them, be accepted by them. He himself thought that the fewer dealings he could have with people of that sort the better. It was Society that parted him from Diana in the first place.

But for his mother, if there was a way . . .

The sitting room door opened and Rachel emerged, dressed in one of her fine new gowns in midnight blue velvet and silk. She held two open jewel cases, one containing pearls, the other sapphires.

"Oh, Tom, my dear," she said. "I simply cannot decide. Which of these do you like the best?"

"I'm no good at such fripperies, Mother," he protested, rising from his chair. "They are both lovely on you."

She stared down at them in deep concentration. "The pearls, then. I don't want to look too—flashy."

"Pearls it is. Here, sit down and I'll clasp them for you."

As he slid the creamy orbs into place and fastened the tiny diamond catch, she said, "How very strange to see the Hillard girls again."

Tom went still. Surely she would not bring up the past, the reason for their hasty departure from England? He had managed to conceal the exact

circumstances from her for years, though he sometimes suspected she knew more than she said. He
didn't want to bring it up now.

"Very strange," he said shortly.

"I mean, I suppose I must have known they
were related to Lady Ransome, but I never . . ."
Her voice faded, and she suddenly rose to go to
a mirror on the wall, to fuss with her hair and her
necklace. "Diana is certainly much older than she
was. I feel very sorry for her, being widowed so
early. Being left in charge of her sister."

"Yes," Tom muttered.

"But Charlotte Hillard has certainly grown up
to be a pretty young lady!" Rachel chirped, obviously unaware of his distraction. She adjusted her
necklace this way and that, tilting her head. "And
so very polite. She might do for you, Tom dear."

He—wed Charlotte Hillard? A harsh laugh escaped before he could stop it. The thought of him,
a weathered old colonial, wed to a fresh young
girl who had been a mere toddler when he fell in
love with her sister, was absurd beyond anything!

His mother did not seem put out by his laughter. She just nodded and went on. "Yes, she is a
bit shy. What of her friend Lady Caroline? *She* is
not shy, and is certainly very beautiful, and rather
unconventional. And she is an earl's daughter."

Lady Caroline? Well, she was beautiful, that

113

was true, and most gregarious. Even his own friends in Town, who hardly ran in the same circles as the Reids, were always full of gossip about her. If he did want an entrée to Society, a means to set up his mother in a high position, marriage to a lady like Lady Caroline would be the way to do it.

He would be lying if he claimed he was entirely immune to her flamboyant beauty. He *was* a man, after all, one who had spent years in the amoral atmosphere of cold northern colonies. But somehow, when he tried to think of her, of any young lady, in a romantic way, a vision of Diana's dark eyes kept interfering.

He shook his head, trying to clear it of such distracting thoughts. He glanced up to find his mother watching him quizzically.

"Are you so eager for grandchildren, then, Mother?" he said teasingly, their old topic.

"I wouldn't mind, dear, you know that. I'm not getting any younger. Mostly, though, I worry about *you*."

"Me?" Well, weren't they a fine pair. He worried about her and her happiness—she worried about him. "Whatever for? Am I not old enough to look after myself, then?"

"Of course you are, Thomas, and you do it admirably. I just hate to see you missing out on the great joy a family can bring. Your father has been gone for so many years, but we were happy together. I want so much for you to know the same contentment."

Contentment? Tom wasn't sure he even knew what the word meant. That emotion had so rarely been a part of his life. Only in the sunlit days he spent with Diana Hillard in their forest hiding place had he known even a measure of peace, and that was far away. Now, his business endeavors brought him a certain amount of satisfaction, and he was happy enough with that. For now.

"I *will* marry, Mother," he said. "When I find the right lady."

"Yes? And do you think it might be Lady Caroline?"

Tom had to laugh at her persistence. "I doubt it. But I do not have to find someone to wed this very weekend, you know. There will be plenty of time when I go back to London."

"You work so hard in London, though, dear. I know there are no such suitable girls among your acquaintance there. I just think that . . ."

Mercifully, the little clock on the mantle chimed the hour, saving him from any further discussion of his marital prospects or lack thereof. It was time for dinner.

"Shall we go down, Mother?" he said.

Her hand fluttered back to her necklace. "Oh—you go on, Thomas. I will be down in a minute, there are just a couple of things I need to take care of first."

Female things, no doubt. That was all Tom needed to know. "Of course. I will see you in the drawing room."

He left the sitting room and closed the door softly behind him before strolling down the dimly lit corridor. Near the head of the staircase, he suddenly froze in his tracks, sharply aware of another presence near him. In the frozen woods, complete awareness could mean the hairsbreadth difference between life and death, so his senses were always carefully honed. Even in English country manors.

He heard a soft breath, felt a waft of warm air, a stirring in the shadows. He spun around on the balls of his feet to face the intruder—and found Diana standing by the wall, her back pressed to the silk paper. Her somber dark red gown blended with the night, but her eyes glowed like stars as she stared at him, startled. She drew in a deep breath, and her white bosom pressed against the edge of her black-trimmed bodice.

Neither of them moved or said a word. Tom knew he could not. They just—watched each other in perfect silence. And he remembered everything about their youthful love, the way her mouth felt beneath his, how soft her skin and hair were, like silk. Oh, yes. He remembered it all. And craved it again.

Diana had tried to stay quiet, to let Tom pass by, ignorant of her presence. She was so very nervous to be alone with him, without the safe buffer of a crowd around them. Afraid of what she might say or do if she found herself near him again. So afraid that she shook with it, trembled with the fear that her careful façade would chip and she would find she was just the same lovelorn girl again.

At the same time, though, she *wanted* to feel like that again! Wanted to run into his arms and feel the very life flowing warm and free in her veins again. It had been so very long since she was truly alive. That was more frightening than anything.

So, she stayed still, her back pressed to the wall, hardly daring to breathe, praying for him to pass by. *Or for him to stop.*

He almost reached the top of the stairs, when suddenly he spun around, his muscles taut, expression alert. As if he was back in the frozen woods and she was a bear to be trapped. As soon as he saw her there, he lowered his arms and those tense muscles relaxed a bit.

His expression was still just as wary.

She couldn't breathe.

"Lady Gilbert," he said roughly. "Good evening."

Diana pressed the tips of her fingers to her silk skirts, trying to still their trembling. "Good evening, Mr. Cole," she answered. "I was just—waiting for my sister."

"So I see. I was waiting for my mother, but she is so long at her toilette. She sent me away, you see, fed up with my impatience."

Diana felt a ghost of a smile touch her lips. "We are both of us too impatient for such fussing, then."

"We always were."

"Yes." She took a deep breath at last, and dared to take a step away from the shelter of the wall, then another and another, until she stood only a foot or so away from him. In the dim light, the weathered lines around his eyes and lips were erased, and he looked so young again. It was as if the years fell away.

What did he see when he looked at her? What did he think?

"It is so good to see you again, Tom," she murmured, clenching her fists in the silk of her gown so she would not give in to the temptation to run her fingertips through his hair, over his cheek and jaw and throat. After all these years!

He stared at her for a moment, his mouth taut. Finally, he bent his head toward her and said, "And it is good to see you again, too, Di. I often thought of you in North America."

Her breath caught. *He had thought of her?* "Did you really?"

"I wondered what had become of you, if you had grown into a fine lady. If you were happy." His gaze swept down over her somber gown, her drawn-back twist of hair, the red paisley shawl threaded through her elbows. "I did not quite imagine you so changed."

She swallowed hard. Changed? Did he really think that? She was older, true, but surely not so very different. What did he see in her that was different? But then, she wasn't sure she really wanted to know. She had so few dreams intact. "I thought of you, too. So far away, in such a strange land. I thought of . . ."

There was a sudden burst of laughter at the end of the corridor, a slamming door and the patter of slippered feet. Diana stepped back from Tom, away from whatever it was she was going to say. There was too much to say, twelve years' worth. Yet at the same time this man was essentially a stranger to her.

A hard, weathered stranger she felt so inexorably drawn to.

Beware, her mind whispered. *Remember the pain when you saw him last.*

Her sister and Lady Caroline reached her side, laughter still drifting around them. It was as if they brought reality into a hazy dream. Diana shivered and drew her shawl up over her shoulders, watching as Tom moved further away from her.

Charlotte linked her arm through Diana's, and Diana smiled at her sister. "Mr. Cole was just telling me a bit more about life in North America," she said.

"Oh, how very fascinating!" Lady Caroline cried. She clasped Tom's arm with her gloved hand and steered him toward the staircase, leaving Charlotte and Diana to follow them. "I have so often wished I was a man, so I could explore strange lands and find treasure! Tell me, did you ever seek hidden sites in the wilderness, Mr. Cole?"

"Are you all right, Di?" Charlotte whispered, leaning close as they descended the stairs. "You seem pale."

Why were people always asking her that lately? She felt fine, if a bit—flushed. She was grateful that the girls had come along when they did, and yet unhappy at the same time. Odd. "I'm fine, darling. Just tired."

Charlotte nodded. "I know, I am, too. Being in company all the time makes me feel that way. I can't seem to think."

"Perhaps tomorrow we could have a quiet picnic, then," Diana suggested. "You could bring your sketchbook."

They reached the open drawing room door to find only Mrs. Damer and Mr. Kirk-Bedwin there, sitting by the fire with Lady Ransome. Mr. Kirk-Bedwin was obviously telling an amusing story, for both the ladies were in gales of laughter. Charlotte suddenly went very still, and Diana glanced down to find her sister watching Mr. Kirk-Bedwin, her eyes wide and a pink stain slowly spreading over her throat.

Oh, dear, Diana thought with mounting realization—and consternation. It seemed she had more than her own unruly heart to worry about this weekend. It would never do to have both Hillard sisters mooning over unsuitable men!

It would never do at all.

Chapter Ten

*E*lizabeth Damer nibbled at her poached salmon and nodded at her dinner partner, Lord Edward Sutton, as he nattered on about flying buttresses or some such nonsense. Outwardly, she was all that was attentive and polite. In her mind, though, she pictured the dunning letters that awaited her at home and pondered the possibilities laid before her.

Lord Edward was a duke's son, which was surely very nice. A younger son, maybe, but still with a tidy fortune and an estate of his own. Yet he was quite young, his father would never let him marry an impecunious widow like herself, and he was a crashing bore. Elizabeth would put up with a great deal for money—age, infirmity, dullness in the bedroom—but poor conversation and social skills, never. Her gaze slid past him, along the length of the dining room table.

Mr. Kirk-Bedwin—now *there* was a man who would surely never be dull, either in or out of the bedroom. Handsome, too, with just that hint of naughtiness she liked so much. He had no great fortune, though, just the possibility of one from an uncle some day. She sighed in regret. Such a shame.

And Mr. Parcival. Another handsome rake, though not as young as Mr. Kirk-Bedwin. Desperation was beginning to show in his eyes—the same desperation she feared would one day appear in her own gaze. He would be good for a laugh, a lark, a wild evening in the gaming hells, but he could not help her.

Then there was Mr. Cole. *Ah, yes*—Mr. Cole. He was talking with Lady Caroline, a mysterious half-smile on his lips. A lock of glossy black hair fell over his brow, and he impatiently pushed it back. He was good-looking, with that slight aura of adventure and danger, of strength. He was well spoken, well dressed. Most importantly, he was very well moneyed. She knew *that* from her careful perusal of the financial papers from London. He had made a great fortune in the furs and timbers of the New World. Not in the first rank of Society, yet what did that matter if he could drape her in satins and jewels?

He glanced her way, a mere flickering look that she took advantage of by tossing him her most glittering smile. He paused, head tilted quizzically in her direction. She wasn't quite sure if she saw interest kindle there in his eyes, but at least it was a start.

Yes. Mr. Cole would do very well.

She took her glance away from him, back to Lord Edward, who was still going on about fan vaulting. She paused when she saw Mr. Parcival watching her, a knowing smirk on his face. He raised his wine glass to her in a mock salute.

The rake! A real gentleman would at least pretend not to know what she was about. She gave him a quelling frown and turned her full attention to Lord Edward.

Really. *Men.*

Frederick Parcival watched Elizabeth Damer with mounting amusement. Her gaze moved steadily from place to place along the table, and it was as if he could read her very thoughts. *Too young, too poor, too rakish—just right.* Her china-green eyes lit up when she saw Mr. Cole.

It was all too diverting. If only it had not been

quite so familiar. He himself had observed the ladies at the party in just such a way, and he found none to really suit. Lady Caroline was too obvious, Miss Hillard not quite rich enough and so very young, and Mrs. Damer, of course, was too much like him. There was only Lady Gilbert. She was certainly pretty enough, despite the dark clothes and somber hairstyles. She was a widow, not a naïve girl, who could make her own matches, and her husband had left her with a handsome fortune.

She was perfect for him, and he had no qualms about the way she had subtly moved away from him thus far. He would just have to increase the charm, woo her slowly.

He gazed down the table, watching her soulfully until she felt his stare and glanced toward him. He smiled at her, and a tiny frown turned the corners of her lips down before she turned away. But did her hand tremble just a bit on her wineglass? She—and her fortune—would be his soon enough.

As he looked away from her, though, he saw he was not the only one who watched Lady Gilbert. Mr. Cole, too, observed the lovely widow, his face serious. There was no charm written there to lure her gaze, just a quiet, intent watchfulness. If Mrs. Damer saw, she would surely be livid that his attention was not on *her*, but she chatted with Lord Edward. Only Frederick saw where Mr. Cole's attention was focused.

Damn the man! He had money enough of his own. He didn't need Lady Gilbert's, too. He would be better off being of some use to poor Mrs. Damer than snatching away the only viable prospect at this bleak party.

Frederick would just have to do something about that.

After dinner, Lady Ransome settled down in her favorite chair in the drawing room to watch her guests play at cards. Miss Bourne sat with her embroidery next to Lady Ransome, and Mrs. Cole joined them to drink her tea and chat. The soft murmurs of conversation and laughter, the gentle shuffle of cards and click of china cups filled the room with a companionable atmosphere.

Only an eye as sharp as hers could detect the undercurrents that flowed just beneath the smooth, conventional surface.

Lady Ransome studied her niece Diana as she examined her cards and nodded at something Mr. Parcival said to her. The man was practically oozing charm, turning a brilliant smile toward Diana and almost, but not quite, brushing her bare arm with his sleeve. Diana did not look at him, and even edged away a bit. Her gaze darted over the edge of her cards, touched like a fluttering butterfly on Mr. Cole, who sat across from her, and then flittered away. Her free hand came up to nervously pat at her hair.

Very interesting. It had been a long time since Lady Ransome saw her niece discomfited. A long time indeed. She remembered very well the summer Diana spent with her as a girl, remembered the way she floated around the house like a ghost, caring only to play sad ballads on the pianoforte or read alone in the library. Lady Ransome had known something was amiss with the girl, probably some sort of disastrous romance, but she never asked. Sometimes a person just needed time to themselves, time to work out their difficulties in their own heads.

The next time she saw Diana was at the girl's wedding to Lord Gilbert. Now there was a great mismatch, the bookish Di and the sport-mad Gilbert, but she looked content enough on that day. And *content* was the word Lady Ransome would use to describe her niece every time she had seen her since. Always calm, unruffled. Never a wave of passionate emotion to upset her perfect surface.

Lady Ransome turned her observation to Tom Cole, her dear friend's son. Such a handsome man! So very dramatic-looking, with his black hair and brilliant blue eyes, so—masculine. Not like those useless fribbles who populated Society these days. No wonder Diana was strangely overset, though Lady Ransome would not have thought her niece to be the sort of woman so easily affected by a handsome face. What else could it be, though? They had only just met.

Or had they? Lady Ransome studied the pair of them even more closely, watched the way the one secretly watched the other, then turned away as soon as it seemed their regard might be returned. Strange behavior for grown-up people. She would expect it from such silly young things as Caroline and Charlotte. Not from Diana. There was more here than met the eye.

Lady Ransome turned to Mrs. Cole, who was also watching the card players, but with no hint of speculation or puzzlement. Rachel Cole smiled benignly, humming a soft tune beneath her breath. The woman had proved to be a good friend to Lady Ransome, a welcome companion in the quiet countryside, but really sometimes Lady Ransome wondered how the woman had ever survived life in the colonies. She was so very placid and conventional.

"Your son is so handsome, Rachel," Lady Ransome said.

Rachel's smile widened. "Thank you so much,

Mary! He *is* a good-looking man, though I say it myself. He takes after his father."

"Then what a fortunate woman you are, to be surrounded by such stunners all your life!"

Rachel laughed merrily. "Indeed I have. They always took such good care of me."

"I'm surprised your son is not yet wed himself. Surely young ladies must flock to him!"

Rachel's smile faded, and her eyes flickered from her son to the other card table, the one where the younger quartet played. Caroline Reid was laughing at something, her vivid red head thrown back, the diamonds at her throat flashing. "Oh, yes, they do. He has not met the right one. I hope that will change very soon, though. This party will surely be a help in *that* quarter."

Did Rachel Cole hope her son would make a match with Caroline Reid? What a disaster that would be! Thomas Cole had worked hard in life, and was a good man. He deserved more than a frivolous, changeable young wife. He deserved— well, he deserved a woman like Diana.

Lady Ransome determined then and there to find out what, if anything, had happened between her niece and Tom Cole in the past. And to do all she could to advance their future.

It would be so much easier if she could enlist

Rachel's help. Nip these silly notions of Lady Caroline in the bud.

"I was thinking the exact same thing about my niece Lady Gilbert," she whispered confidingly. "She has been a widow for over a year now, and is such a charming lady. Her husband left her very comfortable, but I fear she is lonely, and she should have a family of her own."

"Lady Gilbert?" Rachel murmured. Her gaze flashed back to her son's table. "Well. Yes. She is still pretty. But . . ."

Lady Ransome's attention sharpened. "But?"

"Oh, I don't like to speak of the past. It was all so long ago."

Lady Ransome leaned closer to her friend. "It?"

Rachel swallowed hard, her pearls shimmering. "Before we went to North America, we were tenants on the estate of Lady Gilbert's father."

"My brother's estate?" Well, then, that explained it. Lady Ransome had known that the Coles had humble origins, but not exactly where they came from. If they had lived near Diana's girlhood home . . . "And did Diana and your son—know each other back then?"

Rachel shrugged. "They must have done, but Tom does not speak to his mother about such things. Or about that time very much at all."

"Of course not," Lady Ransome murmured. A

young romance, then, ended sadly in its prime. Now here they were, reunited!

She almost clapped her hands in delight. It was just like a novel!

She dared not get too excited yet, though. She had to plan carefully, just as an expert stage manager would. She leaned even closer to Rachel, and murmured, "Oh, my dear friend, let me tell you more about my darling niece."

"Shall we have a picnic tomorrow?" Caroline said, as they all folded their cards after a final game. "A merry one, down by the stream? We can eat sweets and drink wine, and laugh and dance, all day long on the mossy banks!"

Charlotte gazed wearily at her friend. Diana's plans for a picnic earlier had sounded far more restful than Caro's! She longed to laugh at her friend's flights of fancy, just as she usually did, yet somehow she was just too tired. She felt as if she had run a mile.

And all because of the man who sat next to her. Roland Kirk-Bedwin. It took all her energy not to reach out and touch his hand as he dealt cards with quick, graceful movements. Not to stare at him like some obvious, moonstruck maiden. Not to lean toward him, breathe deeply of his spicy cologne.

It was not like her at all! Usually being near a man just made her want to run away and hide in shyness. Not rest her head on his shoulder and inhale the scent of his skin! It was bewildering, and tiring! She didn't know how bolder, more flirtatious girls did it.

Girls like Caroline. Caro leaned close to Lord Edward, resting her fingertips lightly on his sleeve and giving him a pouting, beseeching glance. "Does not a picnic sound glorious, Lord Edward?" she cooed.

Lord Edward stared at her, his eyes wide behind his spectacles, a faint sheen of perspiration across his brow. Was *this* the gentleman who had spoken to her so rationally about Medieval gargoyles only that very afternoon? "I—ah, certainly, Lady Caroline," he muttered.

"Wonderful! Then I'm sure you can help me persuade Lady Ransome."

Charlotte watched as Caroline rose from the table, and waited with a brilliant smile until Lord Edward leaped to his feet and offered her his arm. They strolled across the room to where Lady Ransome sat in state, Caroline leaning on his arm and Lord Edward staring down at her as if some magical fairy-creature had just alighted on his sleeve.

Astonishing, Charlotte thought.

"Amazing," Mr. Kirk-Bedwin murmured, as if echoing her own thoughts. She glanced over at him. He was idly shuffling the cards, an enigmatic smile on his lips.

Charlotte remembered how he looked sitting alone in the moonlight, so lonely and beautiful, so alluring. "Amazing?"

"I always thought Edward was only interested in his obscure Gothic architecture, that he did not even notice the lovely debutantes clustered around him. Yet look at him now. All thanks to your friend Lady Caroline."

There was a strange, bitter undertone to his voice, and Charlotte suddenly recalled something besides how handsome he looked sitting in gardens. She remembered how he had courted Caroline. How Caroline had dropped him.

A sudden cold spread over Charlotte's skin, making her shiver despite the warmth of the overheated room. She felt very small, and very foolish. How could she have forgotten even for a moment? She was Caro's friend; he must be trying to gain her regard to get back into Caroline's good graces. Men like him were never really interested in quiet girls like herself.

"Are you well, Miss Hillard?" Roland asked, his voice soft and full of concern.

Charlotte pressed her hand to her head, which would not cease spinning. "I am just tired, Mr. Kirk-Bedwin."

"Let me fetch your sister, then."

Charlotte watched as he hurried across the room, bending to whisper in Diana's ear. Her sister's gaze shot toward her, and Charlotte tried to smile reassuringly, but it was too great an effort. She *was* tired all of a sudden, tired and a bit sad. So silly, to be sad for something she had never really had in the first place.

Chapter Eleven

The day of the picnic dawned sunny and warm, perfect weather for being outdoors, for a lazy afternoon of idle fun. Their party, though, set out from Ransome Park in decidedly mixed spirits.

As Lady Ransome and Mrs. Cole chose to stay behind, working on their needlework in the morning room and having a quiet coze, Diana was elected hostess for the day. She organized the servants to bring the pavilion and cushions, the baskets and jugs, and set out after the young people, who had gone ahead to find the prettiest spot next to the stream.

She saw them in the not too far distance, the girls' pastel muslins fluttering in the breeze, their straw hats shielding them from the sun, dappled with light filtered through the trees like a pastel painting. Diana could hear Lady Caroline's laughter, the rise and fall of conversation.

But there was no laughter from Charlotte today.

Diana's steps slowed, and she frowned as she thought of how pale and strained her sister looked last night when Diana tucked her into bed with a soothing tisane. It was not like Charlotte to be ill at all, she had always been so healthy, so scornful of female vapors. Charlotte had just said she was tired, and perhaps that was all it was. The Season had been a strain on all of them, with the constant to-and-froing of social occasions. Charlotte was so shy.

Yet Diana had the sense that mere tiredness was not the whole story. Something else was worrying Charlotte. If only she would talk about it!

Diana knew she could not *make* her speak, though. Charlotte had always had to come to things through her own time. All Diana could do was stay beside her.

She straightened her bonnet and prepared to follow the others along the shaded pathway, but she was stopped by a voice behind her.

"Good morning, Lady Gilbert," a man's deep tone said. "Lovely weather for a picnic, is it not?"

Tom Cole. Diana slowly turned to find him standing on the front steps of the house. He was casually dressed for their outing in buff doeskin breeches and a dark burgundy-colored coat. He held his hat in his hand, and the wind caressed his black hair, tousling it, turning it glossy in the light. He grinned at her, and for a moment she was transported back in time. The years fell away, and she was a girl again.

She shook her head, trying to clear it of the memories, to remind herself of where they were, *who* they were. "Yes," she answered. "A very fine morning."

He came down the steps to her side, and fell naturally into step beside her as they strolled down the pathway. The others were far ahead of them by then, barely seen.

For a moment, they walked in silence, the only sound the rustle of their footsteps on the earth, the whisper of the wind in the trees. Diana fussed with the fringed hem of her shawl, seeking for something, anything, to say. If they conversed, perhaps she would not be so very aware of his warm nearness. Of the remembrance of his kisses—of wondering how they might have changed over the years.

In the end, though, he was the one who spoke first. "You have not aged at all, Diana," he said hoarsely. "I do beg your pardon—Lady Gilbert."

"I wish you would call me Diana," she blurted,

longing with all her strength to hear him say her name again. "It makes me feel—young again. It is very kind of you to say I haven't aged, but I know I have. Some days I feel so very ancient, as if I'll never enjoy anything ever again." She paused, glancing at him from the corner of her eye. His face was impassive, attentive, as if he waited to see what she would say next. She wasn't sure herself what she would say! She had already voiced more than she had in years.

"Like a picnic on a sunny day?" he said.

Diana gave a strangled laugh. "Yes. Or a walk through the woods with an old friend."

"Do you consider me to be your friend?"

"Once, you were my very best friend. I have so cherished the memories. Often I've wondered what your life was like, if you were—happy."

"I have been happy enough. Life in the colonies was good to me in many ways. A man can find his own direction there, make his own place, in a way that is almost impossible here."

"And yet you came back?"

"I came back, yes." His voice was quiet, yet so full of leashed emotion, of so much that was unsaid. "My mother was homesick, and perhaps I was, too. The cold climate was not good for her health, and there was not much society of women her own age for her."

"What did *you* miss most about England?" Diana asked. If only he had missed *her* the most, yet she dared not even voice that wish to herself. For her seeing him again made it seem as if time had never passed, as if they had seen each other only a few days ago. His life had been filled with events and adventure; she was surely just a hazy memory to him. But he was vivid and real to her.

"I missed the green," he said, tilting back his head to take in the rich canopy of trees they strolled beneath. "Summer in North America is very short, the green so quickly vanished beneath snow and ice. I missed the gentle breezes, the soft air. I even found I missed the people."

"The people?"

"Yes. Colonists are a hardy lot, and full of interest and variety. One can't be too bored with them, that's for certain. And yet . . ."

"Yet they do not like poetry?"

Tom laughed. "No, most of them had little appreciation for literature of any sort. They were usually planning their next expedition, or just trying to stay alive. Poetry was a frivolous nuisance."

Diana remembered the long, youthful hours together in their hiding spot, Tom's voice rich and deep as he read her the words of Coleridge and Shelley and Byron, the reverent way he would go back over particularly beautiful passages. She could not imagine him in a wasteland devoid of the beauty of words, the finer things in life. "I'm so sorry."

"It was not as bad as all that, Di," he said laughingly. "I was not exactly banished to the outer reaches of hell. I was sometimes able to procure new volumes, and they were all the sweeter for their scarcity. But I daresay your own life has been quite different."

"Yes," Diana answered, thinking of her Mayfair townhouse, her evenings out. "I have lived in London most of the time, and there are so many literary and philosophical societies to partake of."

"Your husband did not also enjoy the Town life?"

Diana peered at him, surprised at the new note of strain in his tone. Surprised he would mention her husband at all. "It is true that Lord Gilbert preferred the country. He enjoyed riding and the hunt, shooting when he had the chance. Yet he understood that my own interests lay elsewhere, and had no objection to my staying in Town most of the year." That was what had made her marriage a success. The fact that she saw her husband only a few times a year. But she didn't say that.

"I see," he answered slowly.

"I was surprised to hear *you* had not wed."

"Ah, well, there was a distinct lack of suitable

brides where I lived. Eligible young ladies seldom trekked into the wilderness to check on traps."

"There were no ladies even in York? Your mother said you had a house there."

"There were a few, of course. Sisters and cousins of the colonial administrators, mostly, girls sent out from England to find a match for one reason or the other. India was more the usual place for such things, but some came to North America."

Diana had a vision of hordes of desperate young ladies in white, swarming like a flock of buxom pigeons around Tom. She bit her lip to keep from laughing. "None of them appealed to you?"

"I fear not. Now that we are back in England, though, I think my mother cherishes some match-making hopes."

Diana had noticed that Mrs. Cole and Aunt Mary watched Tom while they all played at cards last night, a matching speculative gleam in their eyes. She knew that Aunt Mary loved nothing more than orchestrating romances, situating peoples' lives into what she considered an orderly fashion. Diana would not be surprised to find that that was why Aunt Mary had composed this particular guest list for her house party in the first place. And Mrs. Cole was her bosom bow. Of course she would enlist Lady Ransome's help in finding a wife for her son, a wife to bring grand-children and maybe a position in Society.

The question was, who did they really have in mind? Charlotte—God forbid? Or Lady Caroline?

"What about you?" Diana asked softly. They were near the picnic site now; she could hear the buzz of voices, the bustle of the pavilion being set up and food laid out. She should be there to supervise, yet she found herself loathe to leave Tom's side. Not now, when they were so close to their old ease and honesty with each other. "Do you think it's time to find a wife?"

He turned to face her, his blue eyes full of ques-tions. "I am—not averse to starting a family. Many of my friends are most content with their wives and children, and I envy them that joy. But it must be with the right lady. I have also seen too much misery arise from mismatches."

Diana clutched her shawl tighter around her shoulders. "Lady Caroline Reid is very beautiful. She was quite the Toast of the Season."

"Yes, so I have heard," Tom answered shortly. "No one can deny Lady Caroline's beauty."

"There you are!" a fluting voice called out. "I thought you would never arrive, Mr. Cole. Or you, of course, Lady Gilbert."

Diana turned to see Mrs. Elizabeth Damer floating toward them, her thin, pale yellow gown shimmering around her. Diana could not help but notice that her bodice was rather low cut for the afternoon, as if Mrs. Damer had "accidentally" forgotten her scarf. The neckline was wide and square, displaying a vast amount of creamy flesh and a few enticing golden curls that escaped her coiffure and bounced along her bare throat.

It was ridiculously youthful, even scandalous, for a widowed lady of a certain age to go about so. Yet Diana suddenly felt staid and stuffy in her dark green walking dress and plain straw bonnet.

Mrs. Damer took Tom's arm and smiled up at him, dimples flashing in her rouge-pink cheeks. "You must come and sit beside me, Mr. Cole, for I have been reading a book about the fur trade, and I have ever so many questions! You are the only one who can answer them."

She led him away toward the picnic pavilion. Tom cast one look, full of pleading, over his shoulder to Diana as he left. But she could not help him. Women like Elizabeth Damer were a force of nature, bent on their own ends no matter what, no matter who got hurt. And Diana had her own duties to attend to.

She did long to burst into laughter, though. The day suddenly seemed to promise much more amusement than she had thought it would. If only she did not have to worry about her sister, or the charms of Lady Caroline Reid.

Tom half-listened to Mrs. Damer, as she settled the two of them on a pair of cushions beneath the shady pavilion and chattered on about some book she had read. He answered her questions at all the appropriate moments, and even smiled at her flirtatious sallies. Yet all the time his awareness was fully on Diana, always conscious of where she was and what she was doing.

She bustled efficiently around the pavilion, instructing the servants as they laid out the repast and poured goblets of lemonade. She readjusted some of the cushions, spoke quietly to her sister, laughed a bit with Lord Edward, and generally stayed in constant, graceful motion.

He had not been lying when he told her she hadn't aged a bit. She was still the same slender, energetic lady he remembered, still crackling with energy and curiosity, despite the fact that she tried to hide it behind matronly clothes and a demure air. Her eyes, though, the dark eyes he had dreamed of for so long, had lost a bit of their sparkle. They were more observant now, more careful.

He had thought that if he saw her again, the gulf between them would be so great it could never be bridged. Once they had meant so much to each other, but their lives turned down such different pathways. Surely age and distance would break the silver band that once stretched between them, binding them.

Now he saw that was not so. The band was still there, thinner perhaps, a bit tarnished, but growing stronger every time he saw her. He wanted to hold her, to bury his face in her rose-scented hair and never let her go again. To pour out all the dreams and longings he had stored up over the years.

He couldn't, of course. This party was so very public, so full of watchful eyes and speculating minds. And he could not escape Mrs. Damer's attentions, surely even if he tried! But there must be time now, time for them to be alone together, to talk.

He watched as Diana spoke to a footman, leaning over to examine a platter of cheese and fruit. A long, chestnut curl fell from beneath her plain bonnet, bouncing against her cheek. As she reached up to brush it back, a hand suddenly came out to touch her arm.

Diana straightened, her expression startled, and Tom's gaze swung over to find Mr. Frederick Parcival. The man's clasp tightened a bit on her sleeve, and he bent his head to whisper in her ear.

She shook her head, but Tom could see a pink blush across her cheeks.

Damn the man! How dare he touch Diana, whisper in her ear? Tom half-rose from his seat, only to see Diana step back from Mr. Parcival in an adroit little movement. She smiled politely, and slid her arm from his clasp. Tom slowly sat back down, watching carefully as Diana moved away. Mr. Parcival followed, yet did not touch her again.

Tom still felt his blood run hot at the man's flirtatious demeanor. It was obvious that Diana could take care of herself; after all, she had been an independent lady for a long time. Yet there was still that spark inside him that wanted to be her knight, wanted to gain her admiration.

Wanted to love her.

". . . do you not agree, Mr. Cole?" Mrs. Damer chirped beside him, drawing his attention back to her.

Tom's glance moved over her face. She smiled at him expectantly, leaning even closer to display her powdered bosom. She held his arm tightly, as if to keep him by her side. "Er—yes," he muttered. "Of course."

"Excellent!" She clapped her hands together in obvious delight. "Then I will save the first two dances for you on our excursion to the assembly rooms tomorrow night."

Dancing? Blast! Tom hated to dance, he always felt so awkward, like an ungainly bull. Yet somehow he had promised himself into dancing with Mrs. Damer. He didn't even recall anything about an outing to any assembly rooms. How long had he been staring at Diana like a moonstruck calf, anyway?

"Assembly rooms?" he said.

Mrs. Damer's eyes widened. "Yes. Lady Ransome spoke of it last night. Do you not remember, Mr. Cole? It sounded like ever so much fun, even if it *is* just a village gathering."

"I remember," he answered. "And you would honor me to dance the first two dances with me, Mrs. Damer." What else could he say?

She beamed up at him. "Lovely! I'm sure you must be such a fine dancer, Mr. Cole. I can always tell such things about a man, you know." She reached out for a strawberry in one of the serving bowls, and leaned over to pop it into his mouth. Her fingers brushed his lips ever so slightly. "It's my gift."

Tom felt a sudden tingle on the back of his neck. He reached up to rub at it, and turned to find Diana watching him. Her eyes were narrowed, her face set in cool, disapproving lines. But her lips trembled slightly, and he had the strange feeling that she was *laughing* at him. She slowly shook her head.

So—the impudent minx he had once known was still there, beneath the perfect lady she had become. He wondered what he could possibly do to draw her out in the open, once and for all.

Chapter Twelve

*H**e was never going to notice her.*

Caroline stared fixedly at her reflection in her dressing table mirror, but she did not really see the upswept loops of red hair, bound by ropes of pearls and ribbons, or the web of diamonds and pearls that sparkled at her throat. She saw only the purplish smudges beneath her eyes, the paleness of her cheeks. She saw only flaws, and tried to decide which one made Lord Edward Sutton not notice her.

Oh, he noticed her a bit, of course. No one around her could help but do so once she put her mind to being noticed. He listened to her, even smiled at her. But there was none of that spark she longed to see in his eyes, none of the need she craved in his polite touch.

She had loved him for so many weeks! He was so very intelligent, so good, so *worthy*—he was worth ten of all those other fribbles who flocked around her. He was the one she was meant to be with forever. Why could he not see that? What was it about her that held him away?

Caroline suddenly had a most alarming thought. Perhaps *she* was not worthy of *him*. Despite all the books she had read to improve her mind, her new interest in Greek history, all the museums she had visited. Or maybe—maybe she was just not good enough. She was too loud, too flirtatious. She glanced at the pile of books on her bedside table, great scholarly tomes she had foolishly imagined would make her more attractive to Lord Edward.

Caroline sighed deeply. There had to be some way to gain his regard! She had always managed to find methods of gaining what she wanted in life. This one, the most important goal ever, would just take a bit more planning.

A bit more—something.

There was a gentle knock at the door, which then slid open to admit Charlotte. She was very pretty, as always, though she never seemed to realize her true attractions. Very demure, yet stylish in her robe of silver lace over a white silk slip, white rosebuds twined in her pale hair. She gave

Caroline a sweet smile, and Caroline only then noticed the top of the book peeking out from Charlotte's beaded reticule. Charlotte even carried books to dances, then! How silly and bluestockingish. How very . . .

Perfect.

Caroline would just have to find a way to be more like Charlotte! Lord Edward would surely appreciate her then. Surely see her true inner worth, as no one ever had before.

"Are you almost ready, Caro?" Charlotte asked. "The carriages are being brought around."

"Oh, yes, very soon. Charlotte, dear, do come sit here beside me for a moment. I want to ask you something."

The village assembly rooms were much the same as village assembly rooms everywhere—a long, low brick building, lined with windows that faced the street, and a curving drive to accommodate carriages. Charlotte leaned forward to peer out the carriage window as they rumbled down the street, closer and closer to the lights and the music.

Usually such occasions, even relatively small, casual events such as this one, made her a bit nervous, a bit frightened of who she might see or have to speak with. Tonight, though, she was too puzzled by her conversation with Caroline to be too full of trepidation.

Charlotte had suspected that her friend had some interest in Lord Edward, of course. It was hard to miss the attention she paid him, both at dinner and the picnic. But that was hardly unusual; Caroline liked to flirt with all handsome young men. Lord Edward just seemed a very different sort of choice for flirtation. Caroline had also confided in Charlotte on their arrival at Ransome Park that she had dropped Mr. Kirk-Bedwin because of her affection for someone else.

Charlotte would never have dreamed that the "someone else" was Lord Edward Sutton, though! Or that Caroline was so very serious about him.

"Oh, Charlotte," Caroline had said sadly in her room, clutching at Charlotte's hand. "I am at my wits' end, I do not know what to do. Only you can help me!"

She could help *Caroline*? Charlotte could not even begin to imagine how. "Of course I will do what I can, Caro," she answered tentatively.

That was when the truth came out. Caroline was wildly in love with Lord Edward, and intended to marry him if he could. *Marry him!*

Charlotte shook her head. Maybe that was why she so often preferred books. People were too puzzling. But, then again, she quite baffled herself lately, with all her new thoughts of Roland Kirk-Bedwin.

Charlotte slumped back against the carriage seat with a sigh. Why did her aunt's party have to be just beginning? Why could she not just go home now?

"Is something amiss, Charlotte?" Diana whispered, gently touching her arm. Lady Ransome and Mrs. Cole, who sat across from them, seemed too engrossed in their own gossip to pay the Hillard sisters any mind at all.

How Charlotte wished she could confide in Diana! Her sister had been her trusted friend ever since she was a child, and Diana would surely be able to help Charlotte sort out her jumbled thoughts. Di had been married, after all, she knew all about romantic matters. Charlotte even opened her mouth to pour out her confusion, but she ended up just shaking her head. This did not seem like the time for sisterly confidences, and Charlotte wasn't sure she even had the words to begin to express what she was feeling.

"No, I'm fine, Di," she whispered. "I just wish the evening was over."

Diana gave her arm a comforting squeeze. "It is only a small gathering, dear. We can always go back to Ransome Park early if you're tired."

Charlotte nodded as the carriage rolled to a halt

and a footman opened the door. The rooms were already crowded when they entered the foyer and surrendered their wraps before making their way into the long, narrow dancing room. Caroline was there already, laughing in the center of a small group of gentlemen who all clamored to fill her dance card. Caroline seemed to be having a fine time, as always, but as Charlotte watched she saw her friend's gaze dart around the room, her smile growing white and strained at the edges.

Lord Edward was nowhere to be seen, even though he and Mr. Kirk-Bedwin were the first to leave the house. For that matter, Mr. Kirk-Bedwin was not around, either. Charlotte felt suddenly deflated, tired, as if all her energy had gone toward the expectation of seeing him again, and now that she was disappointed it all just leached away.

"See, it is not so very crowded," Diana whispered. "Shall we find some seats?"

Charlotte had not even really noticed how many people were gathered, which was usually her first observation on arriving at a party—then she could gauge where to hide. It was a good-sized throng, with all of their party and most of Lady Ransome's neighbors and the villagers. No one was dancing yet, but a group of musicians clustered on a small dais played a quiet air as the guests mingled and chatted, forming and re-forming groups and choosing their dance partners. It did not quite sparkle as a London party would; there were not as many candles, and not a great deal of fine jewelry aside from Caroline's diamonds, Mrs. Cole's pearls, and Lady Ransome's ruby parure.

Charlotte found she preferred it to a Town rout, though. It felt more like a meeting of friends, like a place where people were actually happy to see one another and were not just there to gauge the worth of one another's gowns. And gossip behind each other's backs. She did not have the sense of being judged and found wanting.

She felt her stiff shoulders relax a bit. "Yes, let's find a place to sit."

They made their way around the edge of the room, past the dance floor and the buffet tables. They were only stopped by a few neighbors of Lady Ransome, who remembered Diana from when she was a girl, and soon found a pair of chairs near an open window. There was a pleasant breeze, and an excellent view of the crowd, but they were out of the main thoroughfare. Perfect.

Charlotte settled in her seat, arranging her white and silver skirts around her and placing her book-filled reticule on her lap. This was not so very bad, she told herself. It might even be rather fun. Of course it could be.

"Good evening, Lady Gilbert. Miss Hillard," she heard an all-too-familiar voice say, very near to her. She felt a brush of warmth against her shoulder, and looked up to find Mr. Kirk-Bedwin smiling down at her. "I'm glad to see that you arrived safely."

"Thank you, Mr. Kirk-Bedwin," Diana answered, with a rather cool smile. "It seems a very agreeable party."

"Indeed it is. And it can only be better if Miss Hillard will agree to grant me the first two dances."

Dance with him? Flustered all over again, Charlotte stared down at her lap, at the floor, not exactly sure *where* to look. She felt Diana's quizzical gaze on her, no doubt wondering why her little sister was suddenly such a ninny.

"Charlotte does not usually care to dance," Diana began.

"I would be happy to dance with you, Mr. Kirk-Bedwin," Charlotte suddenly blurted. She was utterly astonished; it was as if someone else, Caroline perhaps, took over her body! Yet she found she really did want to dance with him. Very much.

His smile widened, a charming, piratical flash of gleaming white teeth. "Excellent! Would you perhaps care for a stroll around the room before the music begins? A glass of punch, maybe?"

"Thank you. I would enjoy a glass of punch." Charlotte handed Diana her reticule and stood up to take Mr. Kirk-Bedwin's arm. It was warm and strong beneath her gloved touch, and he led her neatly through the growing crowd, careful to be sure she was not jostled.

Charlotte glanced back before the people could close in to find her sister watching her, a very puzzled expression etched on her face. Well Diana might be puzzled; Charlotte was confused herself. Once she was settled in her corner at a party she seldom wandered from it. Tonight, though, she did not feel like herself at all. The old ways did not appeal.

Mr. Kirk-Bedwin procured two glasses of punch from the refreshment table and led her to a quiet spot by the wall. She sipped at the tart liquid, watching the swirl of activity around them, always aware of the man who stood beside her. His arm brushed against her short cap sleeve, the fine wool of his coat catching the silver lace, and for an instant she had a very silly fantasy. She imagined they were a true couple, at an assembly near their own home with their own neighbors.

Of course that could never be. Mr. Kirk-Bedwin

was hardly the sort to be happy living in the country, with a village assembly room for his amusement and a bookish wife at his side. It was a nice fantasy, even so. A moment where she could pretend she was beautiful enough to be his wife, to be the envy of others. To share a pleasant life with him in a place like this.

"Are you enjoying yourself, Miss Hillard?" he asked.

Charlotte blinked, tearing herself away from her little daydream. "Oh, yes. It seems most convivial here."

"Yes, it does," he answered, not sounding at all cynical or ironic. In fact, he just sounded—surprised. "I seldom have the chance to attend events like this."

"Do you never go into the country at all, then?"

"Oh, I do. My mother and my uncle both live in Hampshire, and I visit them whenever I can. My uncle has a very pretty estate, a nice place to rest at, even though he's always after me to take holy orders so he can gift me his benefice at St. Anne's parish!"

He laughed, and Charlotte had to laugh, too. An uncle who wanted Roland Kirk-Bedwin to be a vicar? It was too absurd. Though she supposed the female parishioners would be most grateful to have such a handsome sight in the pulpit every week.

"And how would you like making sermons?" she asked.

"Once I thought I should hate it," he said wistfully. "But lately I have felt so . . ."

His voice faded, and Charlotte stared up at him in astonishment. What had he been about to say? She longed to know. He sounded so different from the rackety man-about-town she thought she knew. He did sound wistful, though. So strange.

"Felt what?" she whispered.

He smiled down at her, but it was not his charming grin. It was rather sad. "I'm not sure I know, Miss Hillard. Shall we take our places? It appears the set is forming."

Charlotte glanced over and found to her surprise that he was right. The dancers were gathering, and she had not even noticed. "Oh, yes. Of course."

He disposed of their glasses, and took her hand to lead her to the floor. The musicians were tuning up for a reel, the couples around her laughing and talking. She saw Caroline and her partner further down the line, saw Mr. Cole and Mrs. Damer, and even Mrs. Cole and the local attorney. It all seemed so very commonplace. Yet she felt as if the world had shifted beneath her feet.

*   *   *

Diana watched her sister walk away with Roland Kirk-Bedwin, an unsettled feeling in her stomach. Mr. Kirk-Bedwin was handsome, true, and not entirely without prospects, if his uncle would settle on him. But she did hear such rumors of him in Town, tales of wild parties, gaming, women—and his pursuit of Lady Caroline, which ended so abruptly. He did nothing almost every other young man in Society did, of course, yet she was not at all sure she liked his attentions to her sister.

Charlotte was a special young lady, so intelligent and sensitive. Perhaps Diana had overprotected her since their parents died, but Charlotte always seemed not quite of this world. As if she was a dreamy fairy-child suddenly deposited in England. She deserved someone who would appreciate how special she was. Someone respectable and steady. Someone of quieter pursuits.

Someone like—Lord Edward Sutton? That young man had just entered the room, and Diana observed him as he stood in the doorway, blinking behind his spectacles as he scanned the crowd. Now *he* was steady. Scholarly, well-mannered, renowned for the lectures he sometimes gave at the Architectural Society rather than the sums he lost in gaming hells. He was rather good-looking in his own way, and he was a duke's son. He was perfect for Charlotte, if only her sister could see that.

But Charlotte was staring raptly up at Mr. Kirk-Bedwin, who watched her as if she was the only lady in the room. And Lord Edward's gaze had alighted on Lady Caroline, and he seemed utterly dumbfounded—as so many men were when they saw Lady Caroline.

Diana sighed. Why couldn't she have a magic wand, like in a fairy story? One she could wave and make things right for everyone.

Make things right for herself.

She saw Tom as soon as they arrived, of course. He stood near the refreshment table with Mrs. Damer, who chatted at him brightly, her blue, gold-spangled gown sparkling like her loud laughter. Diana had hoped that their conversation on the way to the picnic had signaled a new beginning of understanding. She still felt the old attraction, stronger than ever. Did she dare hope he did, too?

It seemed now he did not. He hadn't even looked at her when she entered the room, so engrossed was he in his conversation with Mrs. Damer. She knew his mother hoped he would settle on a lady like Lady Caroline—young and well-dowered, pretty, and, well, *young*. With two such vivid ladies in his view as Lady Caroline and Mrs. Damer, why would he look at his long-ago love?

Diana suddenly felt old and tired.

"Are you not dancing, Lady Gilbert?" she heard Mr. Frederick Parcival say, and turned to see him smiling at her. He was rather annoying, of course. Persistent in his attentions, and an obvious fortune hunter. Yet right now, in the flickering candlelight, he was quite handsome, and his smile reflected a kind of admiration.

Perhaps she was not so very old, after all.

"I am here to chaperone my sister," she said.

"Oh, come now," he said, seating himself in Charlotte's vacated chair. "Surely there is no rule that says chaperones cannot dance once in a while?"

"Perhaps not."

"Then would you honor me with the next set, Lady Gilbert? If I promise not to trod on your pretty slippers."

Diana glanced again at the dance floor, at Tom and Mrs. Damer. "Thank you, Mr. Parcival. I would be happy to dance with you."

Chapter Thirteen

*I*t was late when the Ransome Park party re- turned from the assembly, even later before Diana could escape her aunt and Mrs. Cole and go upstairs. She wanted, no, *needed*, to talk to her sister before much time passed. Much had been made clear in the shifting patterns of the dance tonight. Clear about other people, anyway. About her own heart, Diana was still baffled.

She knocked at Charlotte's door, thinking per- haps her sister was already abed, but she heard Charlotte call out, "Come in!"

Charlotte was tucked under the bedclothes, a book in her hands, and she glanced up with a surprised expression when she saw Diana there. "Di! Is everything all right?"

"Of course, dear," Diana said, giving Charlotte

163

a reassuring smile as she shut the door softly behind her. "I just wanted to say good night before I went to bed."

Charlotte slowly lowered her book. "Certainly. I'm glad you did. This house party has been so very busy we've scarcely had time to take a breath since we got to Ransome Park."

Diana perched on the edge of the bed next to her sister, smoothing the edge of the sheets between her fingers. "Have you been quite well, Charlotte? You have seemed rather preoccupied."

Charlotte did not quite meet her gaze. Instead she fussed with finding a marker for her book and placing it carefully on her bedside table. "What do you mean, Di? I am in perfect health."

"Yes, that is true, but it seems as if something has been weighing on your mind of late. I hope you know you can always talk to me about anything at all."

"I, well, I just . . ." Charlotte's brow furrowed, as she seemed to wrestle with her inner thoughts. Finally, she nodded, and leaned against Diana's shoulder with a sigh. "Oh, Di. Did you ever have feelings for someone you never thought you could think of that way? Someone where you know there is no hope, that it's completely unsuitable and he'll never think of *you* that way in return?

But still you can't help yourself, or make it go away. It just grows and grows."

Diana put her arm around her sister and hugged her close in silence. Her heart ached as she watched the tears trickle down Charlotte's cheeks. Ached because she knew what Charlotte was going through, and because there was really no help for it. First love was first love, a wild, unstoppable flood of emotion. And when that love was for a man like Roland Kirk-Bedwin—or Thomas Cole—it was doubly difficult.

"Oh, my dear," she murmured, gently smoothing Charlotte's hair.

"I'm not putting it very well," Charlotte said, her voice muffled in Diana's shoulder. "I can't explain it."

"It's all right. I know exactly what you mean. I was seventeen once myself."

"You were in love with your husband like this?" Charlotte's tone was most astonished.

Diana almost laughed. In wild love with her blustery, red-faced, good-hearted Gilbert? "No. There was a gentleman I knew before I married, when I was about your age. We could not wed, but my heart beat faster whenever I saw him. The world seemed so much brighter, more joyful, just because he was in it. We did not even have to speak. I was just happy to be near him."

And she was *still* just happy to be near him. The room still grew brighter, flooded with golden sunlight, whenever he walked in. Her heart was still just as foolish as it had been twelve years ago.

Charlotte lifted her head, staring at Diana as if she had never seen her before. "Yes. That's exactly the way it feels. I never thought *you* had such a romance, Di."

Diana gave her a smile. "You were only a small child when it happened, Charlotte. There's a lot about me you don't know."

"There's a lot I don't know about so many things."

"You're young. Surely you'll learn in time. Right now, though, you have your feelings for Mr. Kirk-Bedwin to contend with. It *is* Mr. Kirk-Bedwin, is it not?"

Charlotte groaned, and fell down to hide her face among the pillows. "Is it so obvious, then?"

"Only to me, because I know you so well."

"I'm sure he's just being nice to me to get close to Caroline again, but she cares nothing for him. I wouldn't, either; in London he just seemed like so many other young men. Always in a scrape, always dashing about. But here he seems—I don't know. Different somehow. When he talks to me, looks at me, I just . . ." She shivered. "He's *different*, Di."

Diana didn't know what to say to her. She had little faith that Mr. Kirk-Bedwin had made a true, permanent change. Surely he had come to Ransome Park in pursuit of Caroline, but that young lady appeared to have transferred her affections elsewhere, to a man as unsuitable for her as Mr. Kirk-Bedwin seemed for Charlotte. Then again, perhaps Diana was underestimating her sister. Charlotte was very pretty, but more than that she was good and kind and smart. Such things could be powerful. They could change hearts.

She still did not think Mr. Kirk-Bedwin was good enough for her sister. Yet if he did have feelings for Charlotte, if her feelings for him were genuine and long lasting, Diana did not want to see them parted and forced into more "suitable" matches, as she had been. She didn't want Charlotte to spend her life in what-ifs.

Diana would just have to be sure the young man was sincere in his attentions.

"I trust you, Charlotte," she said softly. "If you feel he has made a change, perhaps he has. I have no quarrel with your being friends with him now. Just be very, very careful, my dear."

"Of course," Charlotte said indignantly. "I am not a complete ninny. I won't ever be alone with him or anything silly like that."

Diana laughed. "I know you aren't a ninny!

And will you come to me if things appear to be—progressing?"

"Yes, you know I will. No dashes to Gretna Green for me."

"I'm glad to hear it." Diana kissed her sister's cheek, and tucked the sheets neatly around her before standing up. "Now, get some sleep. Aunt Mary mentioned something about archery tomorrow."

"You sleep, too, Di. And thank you."

"For what?"

"For being the best of sisters."

Diana smiled down at her. "Good night, Charlotte."

"Good night."

Once Charlotte's door was shut behind her, Diana turned toward her own room, but she knew she would not be able to sleep for a long while. Her mind was too full. Full of thoughts and concerns for Charlotte, memories of her own youthful romance. Instead of turning toward her chamber she moved down the corridor to the staircase, remembering Aunt Mary's well-stocked library. Surely there would be something dull enough there to lull her to sleep.

A fire still crackled in the library grate, snapping merrily and casting a warm orange glow into the corners of the room. It was not a vast chamber, but the shelves stretched from floor to ceiling, filled with inviting leather-bound volumes. Along the wood-paneled walls there were more objects from Ransome Park's eccentric medieval collection, things Lord Ransome had no other place for, such as suits of armor and tall, faded shields and lances. Mercifully, there were no other weapons displayed, just paintings of battlefields and chivalrous scenes. The furniture was all old and comfortable, deep chairs and settees upholstered in forest green velvet, scarred mahogany tables holding a wealth of small boxes and figurines.

It seemed just the place Diana needed, a calm, dark refuge in the midst of chaos. She stepped closer to the shelved, tilting back her head to scan the titles. *Courtly Love in the Middle Ages; The Roles of the Romanesque Cloister; The Battle of Hastings.* No—not exactly what she was looking for tonight. On one of the higher shelves she saw another row of books—*Lady Annabella's Secret, The Sheikh's Harem, Castle of St. Giles.*

Yes. That was it.

Diana dragged a tall footstool over to the shelf and clambered up on it, holding the hem of her gown out of the way. She stretched her fingertips toward the sheikh's harem, teetering a bit as she could not quite reach it. . . .

"Di! Be careful!"

The sudden shout startled her, and she lost her balance, falling backward from her perch. "Ahhh!" she cried, certain she was about to crush her head on the parquet floor. Her feet had just barely left the edge of the stool when she felt strong arms close around her waist, holding her safely in midair.

She twisted around, and found herself staring into Tom Cole's blue eyes. His clasp tightened around her, and her heart beat even faster, pounding frantically in her breast. *Not* from fear of falling, though.

It felt so very good to be in his arms, so right. Their bodies fit together perfectly, their breath mingled for one instant out of time. She had a sudden vision of the dance they had not shared tonight, of all the dances they had not shared over the years. All the nights they had not spent in the same bed. She almost wept with the waste of it all.

But he *was* here now. They were together. Every moment was so vitally precious.

Diana wound her arms around his neck, holding on to him as tightly as she could. As if he was not real, as if he could escape her again.

"Thank you for catching me," she whispered in his ear.

"I'm sorry I startled you," he answered, his

voice rough. As if he, too, did not believe this moment was real. "I thought you were about to fall."

And so she had—right back into insane love with him. The moment she saw him again. "You're out very late."

"I couldn't sleep. I thought maybe a book would help."

"Yes. Me, too."

He slowly lowered her to the floor, yet still his arms were around her, still she clung to him. Her fingertips skimmed over the cool silk of his hair, the skin of his neck. How warm he was, how alive. It made her frozen heart pulse again.

"Oh, Tom," she murmured. "How I have missed you!"

"Diana," he groaned. "I thought of you so many times over the years. You were what kept me alive in the wilderness, thinking of you, wondering where you were, what your life was like. Longing to see you again."

"I know, I know. I tried to tell myself I had forgotten you, that you were in the past and I was content with my life. Then I saw you again, and it was as if not even a day had gone by!" Diana cried, all her emotions pouring heedlessly forth. Perhaps it was the late hour, or her talk with

171

Charlotte about unsuitable loves, but the dam had weakened and snapped. She could not hold it in for a moment longer.

"I feared you would have changed beyond recognition when I saw you again, Di."

"I had changed—until you came back. Now I'm myself again. I'm your Di."

Tom groaned, and lowered his lips to hers. It was the same as their long-ago stolen kisses in the woods, the same in that their lips fit together as if they remembered. Yet it was also—different. Tom was no longer a boy, and his kiss was more practiced, more knowledgeable, more knowing. It was sweet and hot and perfect. Diana went up on tiptoe to be closer, until she did not know where she ended and he began. Never had she known such need, such perfection.

Slowly, their lips parted, and his kisses trailed to her cheek, her temple, into her loosened hair. "Oh, Tom," she sighed, holding on to him so she would not fall. "I am so glad you're home again."

Tom laughed darkly, the sound echoing through her whole body. "Good God, so am I."

"You won't leave again?"

"Oh, no, Di. I never could. And if I did . . ."

"You would take me with you?"

"Always, Diana. Always."

"Tom?"

"Yes?"

"Stay with me tonight."

It was very late indeed when Tom and Diana left the library, hand in hand, laughing softly as they crept up the stairs. They were so deeply wrapped in each other that they did not see the other couple lurking in the corridor shadows.

Frederick Parcival and Elizabeth Damer stared after the romantic pair, shocked into silence, suddenly chilled despite the passionate interlude they themselves had just passed in Mrs. Damer's chamber.

"Oh," Elizabeth breathed. "This is not good, Freddy."

"No," he agreed tightly. "Not good at all."

Chapter Fourteen

The day of the archery tournament was not as clear and warm as the morning of the picnic. The sky was a pale, pearly gray, clouds filtering the light and turning the air cool and crisp. But the party did not have far to travel, either, as the targets were set up at the foot of Ransome Park's knot garden. Tables and chairs were arranged for those not shooting, laid out with tea, cakes, and sandwiches. Lady Ransome and Mrs. Cole settled there, with Miss Bourne ready to fetch and carry when needed, and from that vantage point they watched the others trail in.

Caroline had brought her own bow, being something of an expert in the sport, and she lent her older spare to Charlotte. Diana, Mrs. Damer, and the gentlemen used equipment hired in the village.

Diana inspected her arrows, running a careful fingertip over the iridescent fletching, yet she did not really see the feathers. Her entire mind, her whole body, remembered the night before. Remembered Tom's kisses, the feel of his skin, of his strong body. She almost laughed aloud with the exhilaration of it all! Never, ever would she have thought she could feel like this again, so young and free and happy.

She glanced over the tip of the arrow to where Tom stood, beyond the targets. He was talking with Mrs. Damer, who leaned very close to him as she laughed coquettishly, pressing her copious bosom to his arm. Even the woman's unseemly behavior could not unsettle Diana today, especially when Tom looked up to find her watching him, and gave her a warm, secret smile.

She almost laughed again, or giggled like a schoolgirl, so she turned away before she could do something foolish. Like run into his arms and press kisses to his darling mouth. Her gaze fell on Charlotte, who was inspecting her bow with Lady Caroline. Charlotte seemed to be all that was attentive, listening closely to her friend and nodding, but Diana saw the way her sister's gaze would flash toward where Mr. Kirk-Bedwin sat, the way she held her shoulders stiff and tense.

Mr. Kirk-Bedwin, in turn, watched the girls

with a very serious expression on his face. Whether he watched Caroline or Charlotte, though, Diana could not tell. And Lord Edward watched no one; his nose was buried in a book, and he seemed to take no notice when Caroline would laugh, or toss her red hair in the breeze. Diana thought she could detect a faint trace of pink on his thin cheeks, though.

Oh, dear, she thought. *What a tangled web Aunt Mary has woven, with her little party!* And surely the lady had done it all on purpose.

As if summoned by the thought of her name, Lady Ransome called, "Diana, dearest! Could you come here for a moment? Rachel and I have the grandest idea, and we want to see what you think of it."

"Of course, Aunt Mary." Diana tucked her arrow back into its quiver and went to join the two ladies (Miss Bourne had dashed off somewhere) at their table. Aunt Mary passed her a cup of tea, and Mrs. Cole gave her a tentative smile. Diana smiled back, blushing a bit when she remembered what she had been doing with this lady's son last night!

"We were thinking we need a grand finale to our party, before you all leave me," Lady Ransome said. "A dance of some sort."

"A ball?" Diana asked. It would be just like

her aunt to carry off a grand masquerade ball or something of the sort on such short notice.

"Oh, no, dear. Nothing so fancy. Just dancing, cards, a light supper. We could invite all the neighbors, I'm sure they would enjoy the outing. There is so little going on at this time of year. And the young people would have the chance to dance some more."

An informal dance, eh? It all seemed too—easy. Especially for Lady Ransome. Diana was almost sure her aunt must have an ulterior motive in mind. But it scarcely mattered, if her aunt was enjoying herself. And Diana was too content to begrudge anyone else their joys. "It sounds delightful, Aunt Mary. What can I do to help?"

Lady Ransome clapped her hands in happiness. "We were so hoping you would say that! Miss Bourne has gone off to fetch my writing things. After your archery, perhaps you would help address invitations? Then they can be delivered this evening. You must tell the young people they must come prepared to dance."

"Of course. I'm sure they will."

Diana turned her attention to the targets, as Charlotte stepped up to the mark to be the first to shoot. She took careful aim, sighting along the arrow. Diana knew she was prejudiced, but even she could see Charlotte made a most fetching sight, with her pink muslin skirts fluttering in the wind, her expression so serious and intent.

And Diana was not the only one to think so, either. From the corner of her eye, she saw Mr. Kirk-Bedwin sit up straight in his chair, his whole body turned toward Charlotte as he watched her.

So, Diana thought. *It is not Lady Caroline after all.*

Charlotte let her arrow fly, and it landed with a solid *thwack* directly in the middle of the target. She turned with a merry smile, her gaze immediately seeking Mr. Kirk-Bedwin. That gentleman jumped from his seat, wildly applauding, and Charlotte's smile widened.

Diana sighed as she watched this little interplay. He did seem to admire Charlotte now—yet what would happen when they returned to London? Diana would not for all the world see her sister hurt, as she herself had once been.

"Lady Ransome, Mrs. Cole," she heard Mr. Parcival say, and turned her attention from Charlotte to see him seating himself in Miss Bourne's vacant chair. "A lovely day for a bit of archery! But are you not shooting, Lady Gilbert? Surely Diana the Huntress would win all before her."

Diana laughed, for Mr. Parcival's flowery compliments were really too amusing. And, somehow, everything seemed lighter today. Funnier. "I will after the young people have their turns. I fear I am not very proficient at the sport."

"Well, I would be most happy to help you with your—aim. At any time you choose." He stared deeply into her eyes, until Diana longed to laugh again.

"Thank you, Mr. Parcival," she answered lightly. "I will keep that in mind."

Blast, but Frederick had lost her. She conversed with him, even laughed with him, and seemed flattered by his compliments, but he knew she scarcely noticed him. Not like at the assembly last night. All of Lady Gilbert's attention today was now for that parvenu Cole. He remembered how she looked last night as she whispered with Cole in the dark corridor, the way they leaned into each other, fit together.

Frederick did not care what the widow did in her private moments, but, blast it all, it was just not fair! They *both* had money. Why should their fortunes be combined and people in penury, such as himself and Lizzie, be left behind?

His gaze slid over to Elizabeth Damer now, watching dispassionately as she flirted madly with Cole. She tossed her blond curls, posing so as to set her white bosom off to best advantage. Frederick knew very well how lovely Elizabeth Damer was, and how—persuasive she could be when she chose. Yet Tom Cole appeared not even to notice her attributes. He was polite to her, far too polite to walk away or give her the cut direct, but his attention kept wandering past her and her breasts. Landing directly on Lady Gilbert.

Frederick glanced speculatively at Diana, to find her watching her aunt, seemingly listening closely to Lady Ransome's plans for a dance party. There was a faraway look in her eyes, though, a secret little half-smile on her lips.

This would not do. Frederick was not usually one to press his attentions on a lady when she was not interested, but neither was he one to give in to defeat easily. His situation was becoming dire, and Lady Gilbert was his nearest hope.

Something had to be done.

"We have to do something!" Elizabeth Damer cried, clinging to Frederick's arm as they strolled the garden paths, far from the others who were all gathered for sandwiches and lemonade. She tried to smile pleasantly, to remember to walk slowly so her gown flowed attractively around her, in case anyone was watching. She could not reveal how her blood ran hot with desperation, how she saw her best chance slipping away.

"Do something?" Frederick asked quietly, his tone heavy with puzzlement, as if he had no idea what she meant. *The liar*. He was quite as needy as she was, if not more so.

"About Lady Gilbert and Mr. Cole. It is not fair that they have so much, and we have nothing. Nothing!"

"My dear Lizzie," he said. "Those are my very thoughts exactly." He suddenly seized her arm and drew her behind a tall hedge, where they were shielded from any curious gazes. He leaned close to her, his lips brushing her cheek, his hands sliding about her waist to pull her tight against him. She suddenly remembered last night, her impetuous decision to invite him into her bed—his performance there that made her not regret her decision.

If only *he* had money, she thought wistfully. How easy life would be then.

But, alas, he did not have a bean, and neither did she. They had to keep their attention on those who did—Lady Gilbert and Mr. Cole.

That didn't mean they could not spend a *little* time together, though.

Elizabeth looped her arms around Frederick's neck and moved even closer to him. "So, Freddy darling," she whispered. "What is your plan?"

Chapter Fifteen

*C*aroline took careful aim at her target, balancing the bow against her shoulder. Much to her chagrin, she found that it trembled. She was usually so accomplished at archery! Usually loved the martial pleasure of letting an arrow fly, hearing it sink into the heart of the target. What was wrong with her today, when she could not even take aim?

Yet she knew what was wrong. Lord Edward Sutton. He sat nearby, close enough to watch her, to appreciate the attractive picture she made with her bow. He *read*, though, never taking his eyes from the book he held close to his nose. She had thought, after they danced last night, after they played cards and talked and walked together, that he finally noticed her. Finally realized that she was the lady for him.

Now he was reading!

Caroline had the strongest urge to fling her bow down, to stomp her feet and wail, as she had as a child. Then, her tantrums had usually gained her what she wanted, a sweet or a new doll. She had a feeling that now throwing a fit would be detrimental to her plans. Lord Edward would never see her as mature and intelligent if he witnessed her in a temper tantrum! Still, crying and screaming had its appeal right now.

She sighted down her arrow and let it fly free, hardly caring where it landed. Indeed, it came to rest several inches south of Charlotte's perfectly centered shot, and Caroline knew she had lost that day.

She did so hate to lose.

Caroline turned away from the target. Charlotte and Mr. Kirk-Bedwin were strolling toward the tables set up in the shade, where servants scurried about replenishing refreshments. Lady Ransome and Mrs. Cole were there, along with Mr. Cole and Lady Gilbert. Of Mrs. Damer and Mr. Parcival there was no sign. Caroline reached down to pick up her discarded quiver.

When she straightened, she found Lord Edward

standing right beside her, his book tucked beneath his arm.

"Oh!" she gasped in surprise, falling back a step. How had he come upon her so quietly? She thought she was always keenly aware of where he was.

"I'm sorry I startled you," he said, reaching out to take the quiver from her. He slung it back over his shoulder.

"No, it's fine, I just . . ." She took in a deep breath. "It's fine."

"I wanted to compliment you on your archery form," he said. "You are very—deft, Lady Caroline."

Deft? Caroline suddenly felt a warm glow ignite and kindle in her heart. It was not the most grandiose compliment she had ever received, but it was the sweetest. Certainly the most welcome. "Thank you, Lord Edward. I was very off today, I fear. Somehow my aim would not go straight. You must have seen how much more accurate Miss Hillard was."

He nodded. "Miss Hillard was very good, too. But you, Lady Caroline, seem born to hold a bow. Like Artemis."

The glow grew, flaming in hope and need. "Artemis? Truly?"

He nodded shyly. "Yes. You looked exactly like

an ancient statue I saw once in Italy. I—perhaps you would care to show me something of archery after you have had some refreshment? I have always wanted to learn."

"I would be very happy to help you, Lord Edward."

He nodded again, and held out his arm to escort her to the tables. Caroline slid her hand over his sleeve, and gave herself a secret little smile. So, sometimes a tantrum would not work. But a fine Grecian figure was *always* an asset.

Edward hardly knew what had come over him. One moment he had been buried in his book, trying not to stare at Lady Caroline, trying not to make a fool of himself. The next he found himself right beside her, asking if she would help him with his archery.

Archery! Him, who had never picked up a bow in his life, who would scarcely know which end of the thing was up. The smile that lit up her face when he asked, though, made him resolve to shoot arrows a hundred times a day if it made her happy.

Now she held on to his arm as they strolled across the garden, her hand soft and warm on his sleeve, her red head close to his shoulder. He could scarcely believe it all.

When she first paid such attention to him here at Ransome Park, he had half-suspected she was making a May game of him. She was Lady Caroline Reid, after all, the most sought after lady of the Season, the object of every young man's desire. And he—well, he was *him.* Just Edward. Not a handsome future duke like his eldest brother, George, or a celebrated war hero like his next brother, Henry. He was the youngest, the one always buried in books, in worlds other than the one around him. A lady like Lady Caroline could be the object of dreams in such a world, a medieval princess, a fairy queen.

But she paid him such attention, smiling at him, sitting beside him, putting him at ease by talking about history and books. Kindness and interest shone in her lovely eyes, in her whole manner as she looked at him. He quit being suspicious that she was making a joke of him, and just enjoyed being with her. She was not at all the frivolous girl he once thought her.

Dared he have hope? Dared he begin to imagine that she might even accept him were he to make an offer? Never before had he thought he could have such a wife, that they could live together happily, spend their evenings in each other's company, parties at each other's side. He could even take her to Italy, to show her that statue of Artemis!

On a lovely day like this, with her touch on his arm, her perfume surrounding his senses, *anything* seemed possible.

Roland watched his friend cross the garden with Lady Caroline, a faint astonishment growing in his mind. Astonishment both at the couple they made, these two people who he would never have imagined could make a match yet somehow seemed to look so well, so right together, and at something else. At the way he felt when he saw Lady Caroline smile at Edward as if all the sun had gathered in her heart.

Once, all his own hopes were pinned on her. Hopes that he would not have to give in to his uncle, hopes that he could have his wild Town life forever, with a dashing wife at his side. When she dropped him, he had been so very angry.

Now he could not even remember why that was. Could not remember why he found Lady Caroline's vivid beauty so desirable, a London life so needful. It all seemed like something that happened to another person. How could so much change in only a few days?

"Would you care for some lemonade, Mr. Kirk-Bedwin?" Miss Hillard asked.

He glanced down at her, at the luminescence of her green eyes, her gentle smile. And he knew.

Yes—things *could* change in only a few days. They could change in a moment.

"Thank you, Miss Hillard," he murmured. She handed him a cool glass, and their bare fingers brushed. Her eyes widened, and he longed to clasp her hand, to hold it close to his heart and never let it go.

He had to let her go, though, for they stood near the others, near enough to hear the hum of their conversation. He watched as her gaze dropped from his, as she reached for her own glass and took a careful sip.

"Do you mind very much, Mr. Kirk-Bedwin?" she whispered.

"Mind?" Roland said, bewildered. Mind what? Mind watching her, holding her hand, standing near her? Never.

She looked back over her shoulder, to where Edward and Lady Caroline stood together. "Mind that Lady Caroline's—attentions have focused on Lord Edward. I know that you admired her."

Roland understood then. She thought he still cherished a *tendre* for Lady Caroline. How could he explain to her how his feelings had changed? How he could no longer see any woman but her, Charlotte. "I did once admire Lady Caroline," he said slowly. "But I have found for some time that my feelings toward her have been only those of friendship. She and I are too much alike to have suited, I think. Or we are too different.''

''Oh. I see.'' Miss Hillard smiled up at him shyly.

''Do you see, truly?''

''Yes, I do, Mr. Kirk-Bedwin.''

Roland felt a hard stare on his back, and looked back to find Miss Hillard's sister watching him closely. It reminded him sharply that he had much work to do if he wanted to win his green-eyed girl. But it was certainly work he was most willing to do.

''I have been thinking that I must visit my uncle soon,'' he said. ''There is much he and I have to talk about now.''

''Your uncle?'' Miss Hillard asked. ''I should like to meet him sometime. And hear all about your family.''

He smiled at her, and dared to reach out and squeeze her hand in the hiding folds of her skirt. ''So you shall, Miss Hillard, until you are as utterly bored with them as I am. But only if you promise to tell me all about *you* in exchange.''

She laughed, and ducked her head, blushing. Her fingers curled tightly about his. ''Oh, Mr. Kirk-Bedwin. Where do we start?''

Chapter Sixteen

Diana stared at her reflection in her mirror, watching as her maid put the final touches on her coiffure, securing the upswept curls with jade combs. They went perfectly with her green gown, trimmed with jet beadwork at the neckline and the scalloped hem. But she did not really see her toilette at all. In her mind, she saw herself as she had been at that masquerade ball all those years ago, young and eager, so excited about her costume, her first grown-up ball—her first love.

Now he waited for her again, just downstairs. But she was no longer that naïve girl. She was a woman, with a woman's love and desire, and she ached to see him again.

She shivered, unwittingly dislodging one of the combs. "Careful, my lady!" the maid muttered.

"Sorry, Daisy," Diana answered. She closed her eyes, taking a deep breath and willing herself to stay still. It would never do for Tom to see her with her hair awry, after all. She thought instead of the archery tournament, of her sister and Mr. Kirk-Bedwin, of his attentions to Charlotte.

What was the man's game? Diana could not quite fathom it. Charlotte did have some money, true, but hardly the vast fortune of Lady Caroline. And Charlotte was so dreamy, so removed from the real world. Diana remembered the radiant smile on her sister's face when she gazed at Mr. Kirk-Bedwin, a smile Diana had never seen there before.

Diana frowned. If this was some silly game he was playing, some scheme to amuse himself or some ploy to regain Lady Caroline's favor, then he would be very sorry for it. That she could promise. If, however, he was sincere in his attentions . . .

Well, that was very different.

Diana would just have to keep an eye on the young people, that was all. She reached for her golden locket and clasped it around her neck as Daisy finished her hair. The small heart nestled against her breastbone, out in the open at last.

There was a knock at the door, and Charlotte's silvery head peeked inside. "Can I come in, Di? I want to see what you're wearing tonight."

"Of course, dear! Do come in. I'm nearly ready." As Charlotte moved into the room, Diana inspected her gown of pale yellow muslin, trimmed with white ribbon roses and touches of fine lace. She did look lovely this evening, but Diana could see that it was more than the gown or the pearls at her throat and ears. There was a new serenity in her eyes, a confidence in her whole demeanor that had never been there before.

Her sister was not a girl any longer.

Diana felt a pang at the thought, and she reached out to take Charlotte's hand in hers. "You look so pretty, Charlotte. Are you very nervous?"

Charlotte shook her head with a smile. "Not at all. It isn't a very large party, is it? Aunt Mary said only friends. And I am looking forward to the dancing. You look very pretty, too, Di. Is that a new necklace?"

Diana reached up and gently touched the locket. "No, I've had it for a very long time." She glanced at her reflection again, thinking about Charlotte's words. Was she pretty tonight? For so long she had felt old and tired, as if life could hold no more surprises, no more jubilation for her. Were her eyes brighter now? Her lips pinker? It felt like a new day. For all of them.

"Shall we go down, dear?" she said. "I'm sure Aunt Mary will want our help in greeting her guests."

A few of those guests had already arrived when Diana and Charlotte found Lady Ransome outside the doors of the seldom-used ballroom. The cheerful sounds of conversation and laughter, the clink of glasses and the low strains of a Mozart sonata drifted out to their ears. More people were making their way up the stairs, clad in their finest evening clothes, faces shining with excitement to be invited to Ransome Park.

"My dears!" Aunt Mary cried, waving her walking stick in greeting. The oak column was decorated with red and gold ribbons tonight, to match her festive gown and turban, her famous rubies. "Don't you both look splendid? And doesn't everyone seem to be having a good time?"

Diana peered through the open doors to see the crowd milling through a fantasy of candlelight and greenery, fashioned into a forest like something out of *A Midsummer Night's Dream*. "Oh, yes. A very good time."

"So should you be, Diana," Aunt Mary said. "Go, mingle, have some champagne."

Diana gave the room one more glance, deeply tempted. It *did* look merry, and she ached to find Tom, to dance with him. "Do you need my help to greet your guests?"

Aunt Mary shook her head, golden plumes waving. "Charlotte will assist me most admirably, and Mrs. Cole is sure to be down at any moment. You spent far too much time with us old folks this afternoon, now you should dance. Ah, Mr. Walker, our good vicar! And Mrs. Walker, delightful to see you both."

As Aunt Mary turned to greet the vicar and his wife, drawing Charlotte with her, Diana smiled and slipped into the ballroom.

Inside, it seemed even more enchanted. The profusion of greenery muted the light, giving the gathering an otherworldly glow. Diana took a glass of sparkling amber champagne from a footman's tray and gazed around her. She saw Lady Caroline, sitting with Lord Edward in a sheltered window nook. Usually the girl had crowds of admirers around her, drawn to her sparkle like moths to a flame. Tonight, clad in a relatively subdued gown of white silk, she had only Lord Edward with her, yet she did not appear to mind at all. She gazed up at him steadily as he spoke to her, perfectly still, eyes shining, as if the rest of the room did not exist.

Interesting.

Diana strolled along the edges of the walls, greeting neighbors she remembered from her long-ago visit. She did not see Frederick Parcival or Elizabeth Damer, thankfully. Nor did she see Mr. Kirk-Bedwin, which was too bad. She had hoped to have a quiet chat with the young man without Charlotte around. That would have to wait—but not too long.

Nor did she see the person she so longed to glimpse. Perhaps Tom was waiting to escort his mother.

With a little sigh of disappointment, she continued on her circuit, nodding and smiling at the other guests. The room was filling quickly now, and it became obvious that Lady Ransome's "small dance" had taken on a life of its own. The musicians tuned up for the first dance, and several couples moved to take their places in the set.

Diana turned at the corner of the room—and almost shrieked as a hand snaked out from behind a marble column and caught her arm.

"Sorry to alarm you, Lady Gilbert," Mr. Parcival whispered, peering out at her with a rakish grin.

"Mr. Parcival! What a start you gave me," Diana hissed. "Whatever are you doing back there?" She drew her arm out of his clasp and stepped back, placing her empty glass on the top of the column.

"Hiding from the vicar's daughter." He nodded toward a rather large young lady clad in an unfortunate gown of orange satin, who wandered the other side of the room obviously looking for someone. "Miss Walker latched onto me as soon as she arrived, and I had the devil of a time getting away from her."

"Why didn't you just dance with her and be done with it?" Diana asked impatiently.

"Because I was waiting to dance with you, of course, Lady Gilbert." He gave her another cajoling smile. "Come, will you do me the honor? You did promise you would."

Diana remembered promising nothing of the sort. But the music was starting, and Tom was still nowhere to be found. She could not think quite fast enough for a plausible excuse.

"Oh, very well," she said. "One dance, Mr. Parcival."

"That is all I ask, Lady Gilbert."

Tom hurried along the outer walk of Ransome Park's gardens, around the edge of the terrace. He had to run an errand for his mother, which made him miss the beginning of the party, and a servant had assured him that this was the quickest way to the ballroom, through the garden and up an exterior staircase. Ordinarily he would never be so eager to enter a crowded gathering. Life in the wilderness had given him something of a taste for solitude and not many opportunities to practice his dancing. But tonight—ah, tonight Diana waited.

He longed to take her hand and lead her into the dance, openly and freely, as they had not been able to do when they were young. He wanted . . .

His romantic thoughts were suddenly disrupted by a cry from the garden, near the path he traversed. Every muscle and nerve in his body tensed at the distressed sound, and he scanned the shadows. There was nothing he could see—no, wait. Just there. A small movement, a shifting. Another cry, softer now.

He veered off his course, running toward the sound. Even if it meant a delay in seeing Diana again, he could not abandon someone in need of help.

"Who is there?" he called, looking for that flash of movement again.

"Oh! Mr. Cole! Thank heaven it is you," a lady's high-pitched voice called. Mrs. Damer. He should have known. "I fear I have twisted my ankle."

"Where are you?" he asked, some of the tension changing to a vague irritation. It *would* be Mrs.

Damer in distress. What other lady here would be fool enough to go walking in a dark garden in her evening slippers?

"Over here, by the fountain."

He made his way down the path to the marble fountain, still and quiet now in the moonlight. Mrs. Damer sat on its stone edge, her foot propped up, the skirt of her purple satin gown falling away to reveal a slippered foot, an ankle clad in a white silk stocking. She shook her head, tossing her brassy curls back from her face. "Oh, Mr. Cole. I feel such a fool."

They were not far from the house. Tom could hear the echo of music and voices, see the lights flashing past the open windows. Yet she had not called out until now.

"What are you doing out here so late, Mrs. Damer?" he asked, pausing next to her perch. She stared up at him, eyes dewy in the starshine.

"I—I lost something here this afternoon, when I was sketching the fountain," she murmured. "Then I twisted my ankle, and I fear I cannot walk. Would you look? You must have taken care of many injuries in the colonies, Mr. Cole. I know I will be safe in your hands."

Tom *had* seen many injuries in his time— frostbite, limbs caught in traps, gunshots. Enough to know fakery when he saw it. He sat down on the fountain's edge and prodded gently at Mrs. Damer's ankle. It was not in the least bit swollen.

"Oooh!" she cried. "That *is* tender."

"Is it, Mrs. Damer?"

"Yes, indeed, Mr. Cole. Do you think it is broken?"

"I very much doubt it."

"But I am sure it must be sprained, at the very least," she cooed, leaning close to him. "I do think that it must . . ."

Her attention suddenly flashed away, then quickly back to his face. He heard a rustle, a crunching noise behind him, then suddenly Mrs. Damer seized him by the shoulders and pulled him on top of her as she fell onto her back. "Sorry," she whispered. And, much louder, "Oh, no, Mr. Cole! We *mustn't*! You wicked man!"

"What the . . ." Tom shoved her away and sat up, but not before she could trail her lips down his cheek, leaving rouge on his cravat.

He jumped to his feet, and heard a man shout, "Libertine! This is scandalous. Lady Gilbert, Miss Hillard, I am so sorry you had to see such a vile, lecherous scene."

Tom spun around to find Miss Hillard and Mr. Kirk-Bedwin standing on the path, staring at him

in disbelief. And next to them—next to them were
Mr. Parcival and Diana. *She* gazed at him with no
expression at all, her face a cool, pale mask.

"Oh!" Mrs. Damer moaned. "You have *ruined*
me."

Diana had thought it a bit odd when Mr. Parcival suggested a stroll in the garden, a chance for
some cool air after the exercise of the dance. It
had been only one dance, after all, and she had
been very careful *not* to give him any encourage-
ment. But the ballroom was becoming rather
stuffy, and it seemed a chance to converse with
her sister and Mr. Kirk-Bedwin, who had been
standing alone in a corner ever since they arrived
in the ballroom.

"Very well," she had said. "Only if my sister
and Mr. Kirk-Bedwin accompany us."

It had been an oddly strained walk, with Mr.
Parcival leading them down the twisting garden
paths and chatting in fits and starts, his clasp hard
on her arm.

Now she saw why the whole farce had come
about. Why he had insisted on this walk. She saw
very, very well.

She stared at Tom, who was trying to extricate
himself from Mrs. Damer's clinging hands. The
woman's hysterical sobs echoed in the night air,

and Diana heard a strange choking sound from her sister. She herself could say nothing, could hardly move. She could only stare, certain her limbs had turned to ice water.

"Come away, Miss Hillard," Mr. Kirk-Bedwin said, taking Charlotte's arm and leading her back down the path.

"You should come away, too, Lady Gilbert," Mr. Parcival said, tugging at her hand. "This is no sight for a lady."

"No," Diana murmured.

"Diana!" Tom shouted. He pushed Mrs. Damer away and took a step toward Diana, his hand held out to her. "This is not what it looks like. I swear to you!"

"You cannot believe the promises of such a scoundrel," Mr. Parcival cried. "Why, I should call him out for what he has done."

Mrs. Damer sobbed louder, wrapping her arms about herself so as to push her bosom even higher.

Diana had never seen such a low farce in all her life. Laughter bubbled up inside her, spilling from her lips. She could not stop it; the flood was irresistible. Mr. Parcival stared at her in astonishment. Even Tom seemed baffled. But she could not help herself! It was just so very—so . . .

"Oh!" she cried. "This is most diverting."

She reached out and clasped Tom's offered

hand. He drew her close to him, and she buried her head in his shoulder, laughing.

He laughed, too. She felt the richness of it against her hair, her skin. "Oh, Diana," he muttered. "I was so scared for a moment."

"Scared?"

"Scared I had lost you."

She drew back to stare up at him, at his beloved, beautiful face. "Because of this pitiful melodrama? Never! If twelve years and an ocean could not part us, nothing can. Certainly not these cheap machinations."

"Now, wait just a minute, Lady Gilbert!" Mr. Parcival protested. "I have tried to save you from this social climber."

Diana smiled up at him. "And so you have, Mr. Parcival. Saved me from social climbers, that is. I am eternally grateful."

"Here, now! I have been *ruined*," Mrs. Damer screamed. "Everyone saw it, too. Where is my offer? I deserve restitution."

"Diana," Charlotte called. She and Mr. Kirk-Bedwin had walked only to the edge of the fountain clearing, obviously unable to turn away completely from the scene. "Look."

Diana peeked back over her shoulder to see that their little party was not alone. Lady Ransome,

Mrs. Cole, Lady Caroline, Lord Edward, and the vicar and his wife and daughter stood next to Charlotte, watching them as if they were a theatrical troupe at Covent Garden. Which, of course, they might as well be.

"Oh, dear," Diana whispered.

Tom just held her closer, and said, very loudly, "I *will* make an offer tonight."

"Tom!" Diana gasped. Surely he wouldn't. Not after all they had been through.

"You will?" Mrs. Damer said, hope in her shrill tone.

"Yes. An offer many years delayed." He slid to his knees before Diana, holding her hand tightly in his. "Diana Hillard, will you do me the great, great honor of becoming my wife? I love you. I have *always* loved you. You were what kept me alive all these years, the hope that I could come back to you. I want to spend the rest of our lives making you happy. Will you let me do that? Will you marry me?"

Mrs. Damer gave a shriek and flounced away, no sign of a sprained ankle at all. Mr. Parcival dashed after her. Charlotte sighed, "Isn't it romantic?" Aunt Mary shouted, "Say yes, gel! What are you waiting for?" But Diana was only vaguely aware of all this. She saw only Tom. His image wavered in her tears. How long she had waited for this! How she feared it would never come to pass. Yet here they were, together.

She clutched at her locket, and cried, "Yes! Yes, I will marry you, Thomas Cole."

Applause broke out among the crowd as Tom leaped to his feet, gathering her into his arms. "And about time, too," he whispered.

Chapter Seventeen

"*T*hank you, Aunt Mary. It was a lovely party." Diana kissed her aunt's cheek as they stood on the front steps. The wind that whistled around them was chilly, Lord Edward and Mr. Kirk-Bedwin had already departed, and her own carriage waited in the drive. Yet somehow she was reluctant to leave Ransome Park. Once it had been her refuge from heartbreak. Now it was where she had found her love and her life again.

"Indeed it was, Di," Aunt Mary said, clasping Diana's hand. "Vastly amusing, I must say, especially last night."

Diana laughed. Once, she would have been deathly mortified at being part of such a scene. But today it seemed a mere harmless lark. Something to chuckle about with her grandchildren one day. "I'm sorry about that."

"No, no! Don't be. It was the most excitement this house had seen in an age. I'm just glad Rachel has agreed to stay with me for a few more days, or it should be far too lonely." Her grasp suddenly tightened on Diana's hand and she leaned closer. "I will miss you all very much."

"We will miss you, too, Aunt Mary. But you must come visit me in Town whenever you choose."

"Oh, I certainly shall. I expect a good seat at the wedding, as well. *All* of the weddings."

Diana laughed in surprise. There was her wedding to Tom, of course. After last night, surely everyone in a forty-mile radius would expect *that*. But who else? "All of them?"

"Certainly. Has young Mr. Kirk-Bedwin not spoken to you yet?"

Diana's gaze narrowed. Mr. Kirk-Bedwin. She should have suspected as much. He had hardly left Charlotte's side for days. But he would have a great deal of explaining—and reforming—to do if he expected his suit to be successful. "Not yet."

"Well, he will, you mark my words. I have never seen a young man so besotted, unless it is Lord Edward. Now *there* will be grand match, the Suttons and the Reids. A very glorious wedding, if I don't miss my guess. The duchess always was one for the overblown gesture. I definitely want to be front and center for that."

Diana laughed. "I will be right there with you, Aunt Mary."

The front door opened and Charlotte and Lady Caroline emerged, arm in arm, whispering together. With one last giggle, they broke apart and Caroline said, "Thank you for inviting me, Lady Ransome. I had a wonderful time."

"And I enjoyed seeing you again, Lady Caroline," Lady Ransome answered her. "Do give my greetings to your dear parents."

When Caroline had moved on, going down the steps to the carriage her father had sent for her, Diana half-listened to Charlotte take her leave of their aunt, her gaze scanning the drive, the edge of the park. She knew his mother was staying on, but had Tom already departed?

They *had* said their good-byes last night—or rather their "I will see you very soon's." And it had been very sweet. Yet she would still have enjoyed one more kiss!

"Farewell, my dear nieces," Lady Ransome said, giving them each a last hug. "Remember what I said, Diana. Front and center."

"Of course, Aunt Mary. I shan't forget," Diana answered.

"Write to me soon. I want to see how it all turns out."

"I will." Diana took her sister's arm and they hurried to their waiting equipage. As Charlotte stepped up into the shadowed interior, Diana glimpsed a bouquet of violets and a tiny, folded note tucked into her sister's reticule. The hand-writing on the note was suspiciously masculine.

"What is it Aunt Mary wants to be 'front and center' for?" Charlotte whispered.

"Never mind," Diana whispered back. "I will tell you about it on the drive home." They would particularly speak about that bouquet—and Mr. Kirk-Bedwin.

Diana placed her foot on the carriage step, but had to turn back for one more quick look at the house. Aunt Mary still stood on the steps, leaning on her walking stick, and Mrs. Cole had joined her. So Diana and Charlotte were truly the last to leave. The ladies waved at her, and she waved back. It was time to depart, to go back to the real world.

As she slid into the carriage beside Charlotte, she suddenly heard the sound of hoofbeats pounding down the gravel drive. "Diana!" she heard a man shout, and she leaned out of the open door.

It was Tom, galloping toward her, the capes of

his greatcoat, swirling around him, his hair in glorious disorder. She felt her heart pound harder as she watched him, as if it was for the first time.

"Tom," she breathed.

He drew in his horse beside her carriage, holding the leather reins easily as his mount pranced beneath him. He grinned at her. "You weren't leaving without saying good-bye?"

"I thought you had left already."

"Of course not. I just rode into the village to try to find flowers for you, but that blasted Kirk-Bedwin and Lord Edward had already been there and bought all they had. I had to fetch this for you instead."

He handed her a tissue-wrapped package, pressing a kiss to her gloved hand as she accepted it. As she folded back the wrappings and saw what it contained, she gasped. Her eyes stung, and she blinked hard to hold back the flood of tears.

It was a volume of poetry, but not just any volume. It was the very *Lyrical Ballads* they read together so ardently when they were young. The binding was cracked now, the lettering faded. Tied around it was one of the pink satin ribbons from her shepherdess costume, the one she wore to that fateful masquerade.

"Oh, Tom," she whispered.

"You always wore my locket. I wanted you to see that I never forgot, either," he said. "And I never will. Soon, we'll read that book together by our own fire." He leaned down and kissed her lips, a brief salute but a heated one, filled with all the promise for their future together.

As he drew slowly away, he whispered, "See you in London, my love." Then he wheeled his horse around and galloped away, as Aunt Mary and Mrs. Cole applauded from the front steps.

Diana fell back against her seat, breathless, clutching at her book. The footman shut the door and they jolted into motion, each revolution of the wheels carrying them further from Ransome Park.

"Oh, Di," Charlotte sighed. "That was so very romantic! Like a scene in a play. Who would ever have imagined it could happen in real life, to my very own sister?"

"Indeed," Diana murmured, staring in a daze at the passing scenery. Who *would* have imagined, only a week ago, that she would find her Tom again, that they would be reunited? That their love would burn stronger than ever.

Yet here it was. Her very own fairy story.

"Now, Charlotte," she said, turning to her sister. "Tell me about Mr. Kirk-Bedwin."

Epilogue

*I*t *was* a lavish wedding, the grandest London had seen in many years. St. Margaret's was crowded to the walls, every pew filled with the great and the glittering of the land, even Prinny was there, and Wellington, and Lady Jersey. The music was soaring, the hothouse roses and orchids profuse, and the bride gloriously beautiful.

Everyone agreed, as they watched her walking down the aisle on her father's arm, that Lady Caroline Reid had never been more lovely. Her gown of pale green silk and lace set off her red hair to perfection, and the tiara that held her veil in place glittered like the sun. But that was not it, not the key to the magic. Her beauty on that day came from within, a glow in her heart that shone through her eyes as she watched her bridegroom waiting for her.

And, as he took her hand and they knelt together before the altar, a hundred romantic sighs exhaled, and dozens of young ladies wondered sadly how they had never really noticed before how handsome Lord Edward Sutton was.

Yes, it was a glorious wedding, sure to be talked of for many months to come. But not, Mrs. Diana Cole reflected, as glorious as her nuptials had been.

She slid her hand into her husband's and leaned close to him in their pew. Did he remember it, too? The quiet, special-license ceremony in her own drawing room, softly lit by candlelight, attended only by Charlotte, Aunt Mary, and Mrs. Cole. She had thought, as they clasped hands and at long last exchanged their sacred vows, that she could never be happier. She was wrong, of course, for every day since their wedding had only been better, more joyful, more perfect.

And now—now their happiness was complete. She pressed their joined hands lightly to the slight swell of her belly, the harbinger of yet another grand event to come. Tom nudged her shoulder lightly with his, and when she looked up into his eyes he gave her a secret smile.

On her other side, she heard a small sniffle. She

turned to her sister, drawing a lace handkerchief from her reticule and passing it to Charlotte. Charlotte took the square and pressed it to her bright eyes. What a watering pot she had become, Diana thought, since she started planning her own wedding!

Roland Kirk-Bedwin patted Charlotte's hand soothingly. He was fashionably but somberly dressed in a dark blue coat and plain silver waistcoat, as befitted a gentleman soon to be ordained. Diana had not been at all sure of him when he first presented his suit for Charlotte's hand, but truly the young man had come a great distance in the last several months. He mended fences with his uncle, agreed to enter the church and thus provide a steady life for a wife and family, and ceased his rakish ways.

He would make Charlotte a fine husband, just as Lord Edward and Lady Caroline made a fine pair. Caroline had ceased her own Toast of the Town doings and had become quite scholarly. It was even said she was writing her own book on Greek theater, and she and her new husband were to travel to Italy on their honeymoon.

Yet the three couples closest to Diana's heart were not the only matches Lady Ransome had made during her fateful house party. A notice had appeared in the newspapers of the marriage between Mrs. Elizabeth Damer and Mr. Frederick Parcival. Quickly followed by the notice that the newlyweds had absconded to France to escape their debts.

Diana would have laughed now to think of it, but Lady Caroline and Lord Edward were receiving the final benediction. Soon, they would all have to make their way out of the throng, into their own carriage, and across Town to Reid House for the wedding breakfast. Not a moment too soon, either, for the little one inside was clamoring to be fed.

"Oh, Di," Charlotte whispered. "Isn't love wonderful?"

"Yes, my dear," Diana whispered back, her hand tightening on her husband's. "Wonderful indeed."

Signet Regency Romance from

Amanda McCabe

The Star of India

Lady Emily Kenton was eight years old the
last time she set eyes on David Huntington.
She's elated that he has finally returned
from India, but now she bears a terrible
secret—one that could drive him
away forever.

0-451-21337-8

**Available wherever books are sold or at
penguin.com**

Signet Regency Romance from

Amanda McCabe

The Golden Feather
Caroline gambles on a gaming
establishment—and risks her heart.

"An extremely talented new voice."
—*Romance Reviews Today*
0-451-20728-9

The Rules of Love
As the anonymous author of a book on
etiquette, Rosalind Chase can count every rule
that handsome Lord Morley breaks. But when
she can not stop thinking about him, Rosie
begins to wonder if his rules just might be
the right rules for love...
0-451-21176-6

**Available wherever books are sold or at
penguin.com**